Fighting

The cracking of rifles in the barn began to swell to a steady tattoo. Answering shots came from the kitchen.

This was the moment. Heeling his horse, Rocky broke into the open and lifted his mount into a driving gallop. Flattened out on the animal's neck, he reached the front of the house without drawing a shot. His timing was perfect, and when he leaped, he landed on his feet, only to crash against the door with impact enough to snap the latch. He tried to save himself, but he was only pawing the air, and when he hit the floor, he was halfway across the front room.

In the moment that he lay there, he knew he was hurt. There was agony in his left shoulder and a knifing pain in his ribs.

The connecting door to the rear stood ajar. It was flung open with a bang. Joe Bucktoe stood there. He half-raised his rifle and fired . . .

Also by Bliss Lomax

Shadow Mountain
Riders of the Buffalo Grass

Forthcoming from
POPULAR LIBRARY

BLISS Lomax
SAGEBRUSH BANDIT

POPULAR LIBRARY

An Imprint of Warner Books, Inc.

A Warner Communications Company

The characters, places, incidents and
situations in this book are imaginary
and have no relation to any person,
place, or actual happening.

POPULAR LIBRARY EDITION

Copyright © 1948, 1949 by Dodd, Mead & Company, Inc.
All rights reserved.

Popular Library® is a registered trademark of Warner Books, Inc.

This Popular Library Edition is published by arrangement with
Dodd, Mead & Company, 79 Madison Ave., New York, N.Y. 10016

Cover art by Jack Thurston

Popular Library books are published by
Warner Books, Inc.
666 Fifth Avenue
New York, N.Y. 10103

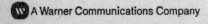 A Warner Communications Company

Printed in the United States of America

First Popular Library Printing: April, 1986

10 9 8 7 6 5 4 3 2 1

Sagebrush
Bandit

1

UNDER A CLOUDLESS SKY BOULDER CITY DROWSED IN
the noonday sun of this July day. In front of Clem
Early's saddlery a flea-bitten dog lay sleeping on the
sidewalk, its legs twitching fitfully in some canine
dream. Out on the sagebrush plain to the south of
town a giant buzzard wheeled high.

The three horsemen concealed in the willow brake
that followed Squaw Creek almost to the town limits,
were not interested in buzzards or sleeping dogs. They
did have some interest in the Wyoming & Western's
branch line accommodation train that had just puffed
into the depot from Keeley and half-a-dozen cow towns
to the north. Its arrival always caused a little flurry
of activity, no matter how few passengers alighted. It
was due at 11:56 and it was only four minutes late
today.

"That takes care of that," said the youngest of the
three men. "It might have gummed things up for us
if she'd been thirty, forty minutes late."

The other two nodded. Their faces were hard-bit-
ten, and there was an air of efficiency about them, which
was not strange, for they were old hands at this business. And yet it was the young man who was the
leader. He had brains; a priceless commodity outside
the law as well as in.

He called himself Rocky Williams, which was not
his true name but served well enough for the circum-
stances in which he found himself. His attire was
shabby: scuffed boots, frayed Stetson and faded overalls. He might easily have been mistaken for a cowboy,
a calling with which he had but slight acquaintance.
But the more a man resembled a cowboy, the less attention he attracted in this part of Wyoming, which was
good and sufficient reason for his dress and that of his
companions.

His battered garb could not conceal the grace of the
man nor a suggestion of tigerish strength that was to
be found even in the lifting of an arm. There was a
mark of good horsemanship in the way he sat in the
saddle, easy and relaxed.

These were trivial things and in no way responsible
for the allegiance he had won from Haze Bender and
Pat Heeney, the two who waited with him in the willow
brake on the outskirts of Boulder City this noon. In
the past year, he had shown them an intelligence and
nerveless audacity that they admired; but there was
something more, something that drew them to him, so
vague and obscure that they could not comprehend it.
It was the force of the man, lurking behind a wall of
detachment that was calculated to impress women as
well as men.

"Hadn't we oughta be stirrin', Rocky?" Haze inquired.

Rocky glanced at his watch.

"We'll wait up a bit yet," said he. "We can be there in five minutes. I timed it last night."

He kept his watch in his hand and focused his attention again on the main street of Boulder City. If he missed being on the handsome side, it was only because his level gray eyes were too intense and demanding for comfort. But he had a crooked, engaging smile to go with them that dulled some of their sting. That hardness about the mouth which is supposed to identify men who lead reckless lives had not yet touched his. Of course, he was young for it; twenty-seven, at most.

Pat Heeney, a thin little man with the innocent face of a child, stood up in his stirrups.

"Not a soul on the street," he observed, with satisfaction. "Been that way every noon since we been lookin' this thing over."

Rocky and Haze nodded. It was remarkable how much they had learned about Boulder City in a few days. For instance, they knew that, due to the overlapping lunch hours, Charles Oatman, the president of the First National and the owner of the Oatman Building and other enterprises, was alone in the bank between twelve-thirty and twelve-forty-five. Also, that the sheriff, Ty Roberts, was home having his noonday dinner; that Pop Singer, the town marshal, was around at the jail, which the town shared with the county, taking over there until the sheriff returned.

These were vitally important bits of information, and they had many others to go with them. They had

3

talked everything over, made their plans accordingly. It left little to be said now.

Rocky glanced at his watch and put it away.

"Let's go. And take it easy. If we have any luck, we can go in this side road and reach the bank corner without running into a soul. No shooting if it can be avoided; you understand?"

"Shore!" Haze responded. He was big and rough and tough. "Yo're right; nobody gits excited about havin' a bank hoisted unless yuh leave a couple innocent dead men behind yuh."

"The only shootin' we'll have to do is blastin' the air to discourage any gents who may be inclined to take up the chase when we're fannin' it out of town. We won't be in there more'n ten minutes."

The side road ran past several warehouses. They were deserted at this hour. The three men jogged by them, riding closely bunched. A blacksmith shop stood between them and the hitchrack at the side of the bank. Ad Hoskins, the smith, was home, too.

"Okay," Rocky muttered, as he and Haze swung down at the rack. Pat was to stay with the horses.

A few steps took the men to the corner. The bank entrance was only ten feet away. A man drove past as they were about to step in. He noticed that they were armed, but he went on, all unsuspicious of what was happening.

The fault was not altogether his. Boulder City liked to think it had grown up. It had started out as a cowtown. It had other interests now. The railroad had long since made it a division point, and with the building of the branch line to Keeley, Boulder City had really come into its own. It had the new four-story Oatman Building, two blocks of paved street, a Chamber of Commerce and even a club for the elite at Cottonwood Lake, two miles west of town. But for all of its airs, men still wore deadly weapons on their hips, when so moved, and you could eat in your shirt sleeves at the Boulder Inn.

Once Rocky and Haze had the street at their backs, they raised their neckerchiefs to their eyes, and when they pushed through the screen doors, their faces were safely masked.

They had had to run the risk of finding a customer or two in the bank. But luck was still riding with them; Oatman was there alone, studying some hastily scribbled figures, and so engrossed that he didn't look up as they entered. His preoccupation was not something born of the minute; it had been growing on him for over a month, and though no one in town had as yet any reason to suspect it, Charlie Oatman, Boulder City's leading citizen, was a desperate man, tottering on the brink of the abyss he had dug for himself with his speculations and misuse of the bank's funds.

He had managed to cover up for weeks, staving off disaster from day to day, but getting even deeper into the mire, with exposure certain and not to be long delayed now.

He had not meant to loot the First National; he was proud of the bank and had built it up from nothing until it was the throbbing heart of the community. More than any other man, he was responsible for the solid prosperity of Boulder City. He liked to think of it as *his* town, and his pride in it ran second only to his pride in the bank. He was unfortunate; that was all. Of late, everything had gone wrong for him. At first, it had been easy to manipulate certain accounts. He had a board of directors—active and retired stockmen—but its members thought so highly of him that they accepted any figures he presented without question.

Having engaged in a genteel form of banditry, euphoniously called embezzlement, against the bank, nothing could have been further from his mind than that other men—masked armed men in particular—could have any designs against the First National. If his mouth popped open and his knees buckled, when he looked up and found the business end of Rocky's gun leveled at him, it was surprise more than fear that agitated him.

"Turn around and walk to the back of the cage and get your hands up," Rocky told him. "This won't be messy unless you want it that way."

Oatman, his face bloodless, stood there for a moment, unable to escape from his trance. His office was located at the front and separated from the rest of the room by a wooden railing and swinging gate. Fascinated, he saw one of the two bandits—it was Haze Bender—hurry across the private office and reach the passageway at the rear of the cashier's cage which led to the vault.

Suddenly Charlie Oatman's brain began to function again. There was a sawed-off shotgun reposing on a shelf a few inches from his hand, kept there against just such an emergency as this. Also, the bank had installed a burglar alarm within the past year. The foot button that controlled it was within reach. He made no move toward either, for in one sharp flash he realized that these bandits were anything but a calamity; they meant escape for him from all his worries—salvation, complete and miraculous and beyond anything his scheming could have contrived.

He wanted to embrace them, help them to scoop up whatever they found in the vault and cage. His hands went up and he flattened himself in the corner, silently beseeching them to hurry.

It didn't take them long. While Rocky kept Oatman covered, Haze entered the cage and swept paper currency and gold coin into a canvas bag. Darting into the vault, he busied himself there in similar manner for several minutes. When he came out, they were ready to leave.

There was a small yard at the rear of the bank, surrounded by a high board fence. A locked door in the fence gave upon an alley. Knowing what they would find in back, the bandits ran that way. The lock was quickly shattered. It was out of the alley to the horses then, and it was accomplished in a matter of seconds.

Little Pat was waiting for them, neckerchief also pulled up to his eyes. He looked the question he did not ask. Rocky nodded. It was answer enough. The way before them was open, and they fled swiftly and quietly, having no reason to fire a fusillade to discourage pursuit.

Oatman heard them gallop off. A fit of trembling seized him, now that they were gone, and he had to reach for the sawed-off shotgun twice before he had it in his hands. He ran through the bank and out into Bridger Street, the main thoroughfare of Boulder City.

7

Down the side road he could see the three bandits disappearing in a cloud of dust. That they could be overtaken now seemed altogether unlikely. That being so, Oatman felt it was safe to sound the alarm. He raised the shotgun and fired both barrels.

"Stop them!" he yelled. "The bank's been held up! Stop 'em! Help!"

It was surprising how quickly Boulder City awakened from its dozing. Men came running from every direction and started hurling questions at him. Oatman's excitement was such by now that his answers were almost incoherent, and purposely so. It was acting of a rather high order. Every time he spoke he pointed to the rapidly disappearing dust cloud, now moving to the north on the Slate Hills road.

The Slate Hills had the Dry Creek Mountains behind them, and then other ranges and eventually Idaho and escape on the broad plains of the Snake River.

The excited group gathered around the president of the First National grew and grew. Men put two and two together and were able to gather that the bank had just been held up and that the bandits were headed for the north.

"Something's got to be done to stop them!" Oatman cried. "Where's Ty Roberts? Does a man have to go looking for the sheriff at a time like this? Where is he?"

"I'm right here," a solid man, with a flowing white mustache and hooded brows answered, as he pushed through the crowd. "Take it easy, Charlie, and let's git the facts."

This was the first daylight bank robbery that old Ty

had had to contend with in over twenty years. He found no reason to get excited on that account. It was his proudest boast that he had brought the law to Boulder City in the long ago. He was no longer young, but he had served the county well and faithfully and his flinty courage and acumen were not open to question. Under his prodding Oatman's talk began to make sense.

"You was alone in the bank, I reckon," said Ty.

"Yes, curse the luck! There wasn't a thing I could do; two of them had me covered before I knew what was happening. A third man stayed outside with the horses . . . You've got to do something in a hurry, Ty. You can use the telegraph and warn the authorities in Keeley to be out to grab them."

The sheriff shook his head.

"The telegraph won't help none. Those boys will be swingin' off to the west long before they git near Keeley . . . You got any idea how much they got away with?"

"No. They took everything in sight except the silver. Thirty thousand—maybe more."

Ty asked him to describe the men.

"I don't know what they look like," was the exasperated answer. "They were masked. What difference does it make how they look? Capture them, get the money back; that's the important thing! Too bad, with a sheriff and a town marshal on the job, that a thing like this could occur right here in broad daylight!"

Ty felt this was unfair. But he brushed it aside and picked half-a-dozen men out of the crowd.

"We'll git down to the railroad yard and commandeer an engine to run us up to the Spanish Ranch. We

9

can git hosses there. If we git a move on us, we'll be in time to cut those boys off before they lose themselves in the mountains."

The wisdom of this was readily apparent; the Keeley branch of the Wyoming & Western paralleled the Slate Hills road all the way to the Spanish Ranch, and never at a distance of more than a mile.

"Git yore rifles and meet me at the depot," Ty told his men. "And you want to step on it!"

The old three-wheeler that had just brought in the Keeley local was on the turntable, being swung around for the return journey north that afternoon. She had steam up, and the engine crew was still in the cab.

"Sure, Ty!" the agent assured Roberts. "We'll do anything we can to help. Come on!"

They hurried out, and Ed Gallagher, the engineer, was told what was wanted.

Ty fumed as he waited for his men.

"Start tootin' the whistle, Ed," he rapped impatiently. "Mebbe it'll hurry 'em up. What's eatin' Pete and the rest of 'em?"

The posse began arriving, but ten minutes and more passed before the last of them had climbed aboard the tender. Roberts got up in the cab with the crew.

"Git this old boiler perkin'," he told Ed. "We've lost a lot of time. Be lucky if we don't git there too late."

With her whistle blasting, Number 12 rolled out of town and began to gather speed. By the time Boulder City dropped behind, Gallagher had the throttle wide open and the light engine began to bob and sway over the uncertain roadbed.

It was less than five miles to the Spanish Ranch, a show place and the home of Hamilcar and other famous thoroughbreds. The ranch buildings were visible in the distance before the sheriff caught his first glimpse of the three horseman toiling over the road, their horses held at a driving gallop.

The speeding engine drew abreast of them rapidly. The men on the tender raised their rifles and let go with a scattering blast. It was noisy and it relieved the tension of the posse men; otherwise, at a distance of a mile, all it accomplished was to warn the fleeing bandits that pursuit was close and from an unexpected direction.

"You're goin' to be too late!" Gallagher shouted to Ty.

"I dunno!" the latter growled. "It's goin' to be close! If we had ranch telephones in this country, like they got around Cheyenne and Laramie, I coulda called Mrs. Warren and had hosses saddled and waitin' for me. I reckon we'll git some of them improvements after I'm dead and gone."

He ordered the firemen to pull the whistle cord and hold it down.

"It'll save some time if we let 'em know at the ranch there's somethin' wrong."

They drew ahead of the bandits, only to lose speed a few moments later, as Gallagher slapped on the air. He brought the engine to a grinding stop a few yards short of the crossroad that led out to the highway, still a mile away.

Ty and his men leaped to the ground and dashed across a field of alfalfa to the ranch yard. Rita Warren (owner of the Spanish Ranch since the death of her husband) and most of her help, sensing that something was amiss, ran up to meet them. In clipped sentences, Ty told her what had happened and what he wanted.

With her usual efficiency Mrs. Warren did her best to outfit them quickly; but there were only three horses in the corral. Others had to be brought up from the pasture.

Ty, keeping an eye on the intersection of the crossroad and the main thoroughfare to the north, saw the three men, bobbing specks at that distance, sweep past.

Helpless to do anything about it, he ground out an oath as he stood there and saw them go. Several minutes passed before he was able to take up the chase. With characteristic determination, he flashed out of the yard at the head of the posse, determined to overhaul the quarry.

They were in the hills in a few minutes after reaching the highway, and drove on without catching sight of the bandits. The road began to pitch higher and higher. To get over the crest of the Slate Hills, it doubled back in several places. On the third of these switchbacks, rifles crashed without warning and the slugs kicked up the dust in front of the posse. The firing came from above and was unanswerable.

Ty got his men through it unscathed, but they had suddenly begun to remind themselves that it wasn't their bank that had been robbed. It had a noticeably discouraging effect on their enthusiasm for the business in hand.

Being an experienced man, Ty Roberts sensed it. He tried to drive them on.

"No need to be reckless about this, Ty," Pete Van Buskirk complained. "Stop one of them slugs and a man could be a long time gittin' over it."

By the middle of the afternoon Ty called a halt; he was convinced that further pursuit was useless.

High in the Dry Creek Mountains by now, Rocky and his companions eased up, confident that they had nothing to fear immediately. They had reached Boulder City by the same route they were traveling now and had had the foresight to leave three horses at a small hay ranch well down the western slope of the range. They found the animals waiting for them. With fresh broncs under them, they rode the rest of that afternoon and well into the night. When morning came, they were across the line, in Idaho, with no telegraph wires to carry evil tidings ahead of them.

Haze Bender still carried the canvas sack that contained the proceeds of the foray at Boulder City. They had food, and they were ravenously hungry, but before breaking their fast, they had a look at the contents of the sack.

Haze counted it out.

"Hell!" he growled, his disappointment immediately reflected on the faces of his companions. "It scarce totes up to seven thousand."

"Seven thousand?" Rocky's tone was icy and incredulous.

Little Pat swore softly. "Why, that ain't nuthin' for a bank as solid as that! The two of yuh musta missed sunthin'!"

"Yeh," Rocky agreed, "we sure must!"

2

ROCKY AND HIS TWO COMPANIONS WERE KEENLY
aware of the fact that the law had a long arm and
could reach into Idaho for them. Since three men were
known to have robbed the Boulder City bank, it became
the first order of business with them to separate as soon
as practicable, each going his own way until they rendezvoused in Denver.

They had the Oregon Short Line Railroad less than
a hundred miles ahead of them. Each reached it on his
own in the next several days. Rocky went north to
Butte and arrived in Denver by that round-about route;
Haze Bender boarded a train at Idaho Falls, went only
as far as Pocatello and there took the Union Pacific
and traveled boldly across the width of Wyoming; little
Pat Heeney went into Ogden and caught a Rio Grande
train through Colorado. Long before the horses they
had abandoned wandered into an Idaho ranch on the
South Fork of the Snake, the three wanted men were
taking things easy in Denver, not living together, since

Rocky still held that to be dangerous, but in daily contact.

A third-class hotel on lower Sixteenth Street, within a block of the Union Depot, became Rocky's head-quarters. He had long since shed the range garb he had worn at Boulder City. He was a conservative dresser, and whenever he went up town in the evening to dine alone at the Albany or Brown Palace, he had the look of a cultured and seemingly prosperous man of the world.

He had no cronies in Denver and wanted none. While Haze and Pat were tossing their money away and enjoying themselves, he began casting around in his mind for the next venture. The lean pickings at Boulder City had been a bitter disappointment to him, considering the risk involved. Little Pat had first sug-gested it and talked it up. Rocky blamed himself for having listened to him. He was resolved that after this he would name the play.

With stockmen and mining men having business in Denver the year around, there was a demand for out-of-town newspapers. A stand near the Albany dis-played journals from all over the Rocky Mountain States. Rocky became one of its best customers. Armed with half-a-dozen newspapers, he would return to his room and spend the greater part of the day por-ing over them, hoping, as he put it, "to spot something that looked good."

It was in this way that a copy of the *Boulder City Mercury* came into his hands. He started to read it carefully, expecting to find some reference to the recent robbery. But the robbery was old news by now, and all he found was a brief statement to the effect that the auditors for the bonding company that had insured the First National against loss by theft had just completed their work and it could be stated officially now that the bandits had got away with $34,109.

It pulled Rocky to the edge of his chair, and he read and reread the startling figures. There was no mistake about it; there they were in bold type—$34,109. And, as the *Mercury* said, they were official.

"Thirty-four thousand!" He couldn't get over it. "I'll say we missed something!"

Methodically he went over every moment of the few tense minutes Haze and he had spent in the First National. He could see the layout with photographic clearness; recalled every move Oatman had made; dwelt at length over the fact that the man had offered no opposition, not by word nor even by facial expression.

Little things stuck in his mind, and he put them together painstakingly. When Haze and little Pat dropped in that evening, he was prepared to give them what he was convinced was the only logical answer to the riddle.

"There must be a mistake somewheres, Rocky," Haze protested. "We couldn't have missed that much."

"We didn't miss anything," was the flat answer. "The dough wasn't there for us to miss. There was something screwy with that bank. That guy was the president of it; we did him a favor in knocking it off."

He saw doubt in the eyes of the two men and it tended to infuriate him.

"Why don't you use your brains?" he rapped.

"Somebody had helped himself to all that jack before we showed up. It wasn't the janitor or some twenty-five-dollar-a-week teller. His name was Oatman, and you can bet your life on it. You didn't see him even start to make a move, did you?"

"But you had him covered," Haze argued. "He'd have been a sucker to go for the gong or the shotgun I saw on the shelf."

"Yeh!" Rocky burst out hotly. "And maybe you can tell me why he waited so long to sound the alarm after we pulled away. We were damned near out of town before we heard that shotgun go off . . . The two of you can think what you please about it, but I ain't forgetting it. Maybe I'll do something about it some day."

"That's water over the dam," said Pat. "Why worry yourself? Besides, we got other fish to fry. And the sooner the better, Rocky."

He gave them a long glance and said, "What do you mean?"

"Haze and me are broke."

Rocky's laugh was disinterested.

"So soon?" he inquired. "I told you to take it easy . . . What was it this time, dice?"

"Yeh," Pat admitted ruefully. "It went faster 'n usual. But we got sunthin' lined up. Not big, but she's okay."

It concerned a sugar beet refinery a few miles out of Denver, and a payroll. Rocky shook his head.

"Not for me. It's too close to our home base, for one thing; and that stake ain't big enough for the gamble we'd have to take. If the two of you need money, I'll stand for a touch."

"We don't want to make a touch," Haze told him. "This job will take care of that. Mebbe it won't amount to more than thirty-five hundred, but it's a natural. We can knock it off and be back here before the wolves start yelpin'. We had a guy in tow last night who works out there in the office. We poured some likker into him and got him to talkin'. We went out today and looked things over. The way it works is like this, Rocky: the cashier gits the money at the bank in Denver Saturday mornin' and takes the ten o'clock Burlington local out to this little station near the mill. He gits in his rig and has about two miles to drive. It's jest open prairie; no houses, no nothin'. The road crosses a little crick. That's the place to give him the business.

"We can tie him up and toss him back in his rig and lead the hoss off in the brush where it won't be found till they start lookin' for him," Haze continued. "It's jest a short hike back to the railroad. We can grab a freight and be back in town in no time. That's all there'll be to it."

Rocky said no. He was adamant.

"That's not my dish. But don't let me stop you; if you like it so much, go it alone."

"Wal, we will!" Pat snapped, angered by his refusal. "Tomorrow's Saturday. We ain't waitin' till next week."

"Okay," Rocky told them. "Just stay away from me for a few days. I don't want these Denver dicks picking me up for questioning."

To make sure that Haze and Pat would not lead the law back to him in case something went wrong, he moved out of the hotel early in the morning and took a room uptown near the capitol.

The afternoon papers carried interesting reading for him. It was on the front page in big headlines. A series of payroll robberies had made the executives at the mill suspicious and they had asked the sheriff's office to have an armed deputy accompany their cashier. The attempted robbery had been foiled, and with disastrous results. Little Pat had been killed on the spot and Haze, making a run for it, had been slain an hour later while resisting arrest.

It gave Rocky pause.

"The fools! The damned fools!" he muttered over and over to himself.

He regretted their passing, but without feeling any great sense of personal loss; chance had thrown them together, and because it suited their purpose, they had gone into partnership. Now—just as casually—chance had intervened again, severing all threads.

Rocky knew that if the police had discovered anything connecting him with the slain men, he could best avoid detection by sitting tight. For several days he wandered about the capitol grounds, watching the house in which he had his room, as he pretended to be engrossed in a newspaper or book. There was a small restaurant around the corner. He took his meals there. Behind his affable smile, he regarded all men with a deep suspicion.

But no one came to question his landlady. When a week had passed, he began to breathe easier.

"I'm okay," he told himself. "If they had anything on me, they'd have been here by now."

The tension that had so sorely tried his detachment began to fade. He went back to his reading, only to find that it no longer interested him. A new kind of uneasiness had come to him. He couldn't understand it; peace of mind had always been his. Finally, he realized that it was his own indecision that was troubling him. He stood at the crossroads now; he could go on as he had been doing for the past year or set his sights in another direction. He had little to fear from the past, fate having obligingly removed the only two men who could bear witness against him. Somewhere, and without too much searching, he could find new accomplices who would serve him as well as Haze and Pat had, if that was the way he wanted to go.

He made his decision, and it was not dictated by any twinge of regret for the past or the moral values involved.

"I'm through with it," he told himself. "I've been pressing my luck a long time."

He couldn't help thinking of Haze and Pat. Without putting himself in their class, he realized that but for a whim of fortune, he could be in his grave, too, or rotting away in some penitentiary.

Rocky wasn't thinking of turning over a new leaf; what he proposed to do was find some less dangerous means of turning an easy dollar.

"I've got a comfortable stake," he thought. "I don't have to be in a hurry. Something will shape up."

Though he refused to recognize the fact, he was already half-committed to a venture so bizarre and audacious that his late companions in crime would have refused even to contemplate it.

He continued to buy the *Boulder City Mercury*. It was a slovenly little sheet, sprinkled with typographical errors and a misplaced head or two. The latter carelessness sometimes proved to be amusing. As, for instance, when what Rocky was led to believe was an item of mining news, headlined "Old Reliable Desert Queen In Production Again," proceeded to inform the startled reader that Mrs. Sam Orlando, of Pumpernickel Valley, had just presented her husband with still another set of twins. On the back page, he found the missing story of the Desert Queen hiding under a caption that said "Rich Dividend for Ranch Couple."

Rocky enjoyed every line of it. Though the *Mercury* was always a week old when it came into his hands, he perused it with far greater interest than the latest Denver newspaper held for him. It was indicative of what was on his mind. If he had chosen to be frank with himself, he would have realized that he was wedded by now to the idea of returning to Boulder City. Subconsciously, his plans had been taking shape for days.

He was moving freely about Denver once more, apparently just killing time. Actually, his mind had never been busier. It was his way to explore his plans negatively, experience having taught him that if they had a weakness, that was the way to find it. But no reason, compelling enough to dissuade him, came of all his cogitation.

From reading the *Mercury*, he was becoming intimately acquainted with Boulder City. He knew that the Bon Ton Department Store was having a summer furniture sale, everything marked down twenty-five per cent; that the new lights were being installed on Markey Street; that Dr. Amos Galloway, the chiropractor, would be in town at the Boulder Inn for three days, beginning on the nineteenth and would be pleased to see old patients and new; that Frank Grimwood, the attorney (and evidently something of a geologist and amateur wildcatter), had discovered some interesting fossils on the Blue Rock desert and was more convinced than ever that oil would be found when a test well was put down.

Rocky often saw Charlie Oatman's name in the *Mercury*. In fact, that was the first thing he looked for. One day he read that Mr. and Mrs. Charles Oatman had left for the West Coast to join their daughter Antoinette at Monterey, for a brief vacation.

It was Rocky's opinion that Oatman needed a vacation.

There was word about the Spanish Ranch. He knew it by sight, if not by name. Mrs. Warren had just shipped a string of horses down to the Emoryville track, outside of San Francisco, for the late summer meeting.

Rocky had once been a rabid racing fan and was familiar with most Western tracks. He knew the Warren silks, maize and green, and had seen Hamilcar run at El Paso and Tia Juana. Otherwise, Rita Warren was just a name to him. According to the *Mercury*, she was confident that one of the horses she was shipping to California, Hannibal, by name, and the son of Hamilcar, would do better as a three-year-old than his famous sire.

"I wonder if this could be the tip-off for me," Rocky mused lightly. He was superstitious and believed in hunches and omens.

When he went out for dinner, he bought a racing sheet. Looking over the entries for the following day at Emoryville, he found Hannibal was entered in the third race at an attractive price.

In those days it was easy to place a bet on a horse in Denver. He put ten dollars on Hannibal to win. Two dollars would have done as well as ten or a thousand, for what Rocky wanted from the race was supernatural guidance, not money.

Due to the difference in time, it was after five o'clock the following afternoon before the results were available in Denver. Hannibal had won easily.

"That does it!" Rocky assured himself. "That's the old hunch I've been waiting for. I'll have a tailor make me a couple new suits. When they're ready, I'm buying a ticket for Boulder City."

3

THERE WAS ONE THING BOULDER CITY LIKED ABOUT
Tony Oatman; she had had, as they put it, "all the
advantages," but she had never felt herself too good
for Boulder City and Wyoming. Other girls, daughters of wealthy stockmen mostly, had gone off to dis-
tant universities and the outside world to return with
their pretty noses held disdainfully high.

Bonnie Wingaard, Doctor Jim's only child, was one
of them. She had come home to find only ugliness and
boredom in the little cow and mining town that had
done so well by her amiable father. To escape it, she
had run off with a traveling salesman. She was said
to be living in Salt Lake City now. Doctor Jim never
mentioned her, but twice a year he took what he called
"a trip," and it was universally believed that he was off
to visit Bonnie.

Of course, it was the prodding and dissatisfaction
of the younger generation, boys as well as girls, with
the old ways, that were responsible for the improve-

ments and refinements that Boulder City now enjoyed.
Old-Timers like Joe Evans, Hank Taylor and several
dozen others, who had grown rich through hard work
and harder living, liked to think it was something that
originated with them. Charlie Oatman pretended to
agree, but he knew that, left to themselves, they would
have been content to keep Wyoming as it had been in
the beginning.

In turn, old Joe and his cronies secretly pitied Oatman on Tony's account. At least, their daughters had
come home equipped to do something if it was no more
than to teach school or to keep a set of ranch books.
(Old Joe's daughter Jinny was the town librarian.)
And one after another they were getting married and
showing some signs of getting over their "high falutin'
ideas." The boys, though handicapped with a lot of
"educated nonsense," were buckling down to running
the ranches and making it possible for Joe and his like
to move into town and take things easy. But apparently all Tony Oatman could or wanted to do was to
paint pictures.

And such pictures! Never anything really pretty,
like a bowl of flowers or a brace of mallard ducks that
your wife would like to have hanging in the parlor or
over the oak sideboard in the dining room. Tony
painted familiar things that a man had seen every day
of his life: storm clouds swirling about the head of
Crow Butte; Indian boys racing their calico ponies; the
Blue Rock Desert, stark and forbidding under a pitiless
noonday sun.

For two years one of Tony's paintings had hung in
the bank. To humor Oatman, old Joe and the other

directors had purchased it for fifty dollars. It showed an overturned chuck wagon, caught in a flash flood at Frenchman's Ford, on Joe Creek, with the cook and his swamper frantically trying to lash the team across.

It was an experience that had befallen old Joe and a great many others in their time.

"It's natural enough," he had once remarked. "You can see with one eye shut that it's Joe Crick. I know that snaky-lookin' gent with the whip. That's Hop Whipple. Used to cook for me. He's so dang mad you can almost hear him cussin'."

Joe Evans had not meant to be complementary, and he proved it by adding: "Pitchers like that is well enough for us around here but city folks won't pay two cents for 'em."

Within the past year old Joe and his fellow art critics had begun to hedge a little, for Tony had shown her work in San Francisco and Los Angeles and had it acclaimed. One wealthy Angeleno had paid five hundred dollars for a medium-sized oil, showing a wise old bronc holding a tight rope on a downed steer and, kneeling on the hind quarters of the steer, a rustler, working over the brand with a running-iron that had just been heated in a tiny fire in the foreground. It was entitled "The Rewrite Man." Oatman had let Joe see the check, knowing his word alone would not have been convincing.

"Wal, there's no accountin' for tastes," the latter had declared. "You can follow some folks around by the money they throw away like that."

But other sales had followed and the *Mercury* had

begun to reprint nice things competent critics were saying about Tony.

"Looks like we got a bargain, payin' her fifty dollars for that picture down to the bank," Hank Taylor told his fellow director one day. "Reckon Tony's goin' to do all right."

"I dunno," Joe demurred. "It ain't fittin' for her to be off gaddin' all the time—California and Denver and I don't know where not—three or four times a year. When she's home, where do you find her? If she ain't up on the Reservation, hobnobbin' with a bunch of Injuns, she's hangin' around some cow camp." Joe shook his head pessimistically. "That won't work out in the end."

"Hellsfire!" Hank snorted derisively. "Fair is fair, Joe. You're gittin' so suspicious of everythin' in your old age that every time you pick up your hat you expect to find Sittin' Bull hidin' under it. What's Tony doin' that we didn't do? We couldn't run cows in Noo York City. We went out on the range where there was grass. When we had the critters fat, we took 'em East and sold 'em. That's exactly what she's doin'; goin' to the source of supply and when she gits her paintin's finished, she takes 'em off where she's got a market."

What they thought was unimportant to Tony. She knew she was the subject of endless conversation and speculation with them. It was true that she was often away, but never so often that she wasn't eager to get back. When she returned from Monterey with her father and mother, after she had been gone for a month, she found nothing changed. Boulder City didn't move that fast.

Oatman went to the bank at once. Tony found him there at noon.

"Mother is getting the house opened," she told him. "She wants us to have lunch downtown."

"I can't leave now," he said. "Mart Ducker is in town about a loan. I'll be busy with him for an hour. You'll have to have lunch by yourself."

Rocky noticed her the moment she walked into the dining room at the Boulder Inn. He had been in town three days, waiting.

"Class," he told himself, not surmising who she was. "I could go for that, red hair and all."

He began to take a long time over his lunch, watching her as she ordered. Her voice reached him faintly across the room, from a table for two near a window. It had tones that stirred something in him.

Merely pretty women never bothered Rocky; they had to have more than that. He had an eye for a good figure. That was basic with him; he never glanced twice at the other kind. But that was only the beginning; he demanded intelligence and fire in a woman.

Tony measured up to his critical appraisal. She had pride and an unmistakable air of good breeding about her—qualities which Rocky always envied in others. Her green eyes and red hair were very flattering to each other. He noticed that but looked longest at her mouth. It was large, provocative and strong.

"Steel in her," he mused, "and sharp claws to go with it."

In his words, he "never went overboard for any dame." But he was interested, and he had not been interested in that way for a long time.

Tony pretended to be unaware of him, without making it obvious. Several times she glanced in his direction, wondering who he might be.

Rocky wasn't fooled. He enjoyed it and wouldn't have had it any other way. Boulder City was small; they'd meet again, and it would be different the next time, he assured himself.

When he sauntered out, he passed close to her table and overheard the waitress address her as Miss Oatman. In his surprise, his pulse skipped a beat and he almost bumped into a chair at a nearby table.

"So that's the way it is!" he thought, as he reached the door. "I might have known!"

He sat down and smoked a contemplative cigarette. When Tony came out, his glance followed her down the street until she turned into the Bon Ton.

Rocky smiled inscrutably. He felt he could congratulate himself on having returned to Boulder City, and doubly so now.

He took it for granted that Tony had not come home alone.

"I'll walk into the bank and have a little talk with her old man about three o'clock," he promised himself. "He'll see it my way."

Rocky was confident now; for his daughter's sake, if not for his own, Oatman wouldn't risk exposure.

He had been in the bank every day since his arrival, using one excuse or another for his presence. It had enabled him to overcome the slightest trace of uneasiness at being back in the First National. When he walked in that afternoon, he was confident and perfectly at ease. Oatman was at his desk. Their eyes met, and Rocky bowed to him. Leaning over the rail, he said:

"My name is William Jeanette, Mr. Oatman. I've been in town for several days, waiting for you to return from the Coast. I have a little business I want to discuss with you."

Oatman found nothing familiar about this affable young stranger with the crooked smile and level gray eyes. He got to his feet and opened the gate.

"Come in," he invited, and went so far as to offer Rocky his hand. "I presume you are a stock buyer from the East?"

He didn't presume anything of the sort. But he had found it a flattering approach that was always appreciated. Rocky's smile broadened.

"I hate to disappoint you, Mr. Oatman, but I'm not in Boulder City to buy cattle. I'm here to go into business for myself."

"That's interesting, indeed!" Oatman beamed on him in his best Chamber of Commerce manner. "We've got the finest town of its size in Wyoming, Mr. Jeanette. And it's going to get better; it's going to grow." He checked himself rather abruptly. "What type of business are you thinking of?"

"Insurance and real estate."

The president of the First National shook his head dubiously.

"I don't want to throw cold water on your plans, Mr. Jeanette, but that field is pretty well covered."

"I know," Rocky admitted, unperturbed. "I've made some inquiries. I can buy the Morrell business at a reasonable figure. I'll do all right, with your backing."

Oatman froze up at once.

"Financial backing, you mean?"

Rocky nodded. He hitched his chair a little closer to the desk. "I'm sure that part of it will be all right," he continued, lowering his voice against the chance of being overheard. "I have some details to lay before you of a very private nature. I suggest that I come back after the bank closes, when we can be alone and speak freely."

It rang an alarm in Oatman's brain. He sat up, bristling.

"That's a very unusual request," he declared brusquely. "I sit here all day and discuss matters of a personal nature during banking hours. I . . . What do the details you mention concern?"

Rocky had risen. Bending over, he said:

"They concern the discrepancy between the $34,109. the bonding company found missing after this bank was held up a few weeks ago and the less than $7,000. the bandits got."

He saw Oatman wilt and for a moment he thought the man was going to have a stroke.

"You'll see me at the door, when I drop back," he said. "Just let me in and we'll arrive at an understanding that will be satisfactory to both of us."

4

ROCKY SAUNTERED OUT, COMPLETELY SATISFIED WITH
the beginning he had made. He was going to enjoy
settling down to respectability; he'd find ways to make
it pay.

The foundation on which he was building was so
shaky and dishonorable that it seemed altogether unlikely that anything even remotely approaching respectability could be erected on it. But that didn't occur to
him; the future would take care of itself. He was even
less concerned about the past. He had looked long
and hard at his back trail and was convinced that there
was nothing that could pop up some day and slap him
down.

Rocky kept Oatman waiting an hour. It was delib-
erate on his part; his way of breaking the man down.
The latter attempted to put up a bold front when he
admitted him.

When they sat down at Oatman's desk, the middle
drawer was half open, exposing a .44. This was delib-

erate, too; Oatman's way of informing Rocky that he didn't intend to be pushed around.

"Go ahead and speak your piece, Jeanette," he said, coldly hostile.

Rocky smiled. "We don't have to start off as unfriendly as that, Mr. Oatman. I'm not here to shake you down."

"That's decent of you," was the cuttingly sarcastic response. "I've never done anything to make me afraid of being blackmailed. Where do you get the preposterous information that the men who robbed this bank got away with only seven thousand dollars?"

"I counted the money, Mr. Oatman."

Rocky spoke so casually that the full significance of the surprising statement did not register on Oatman for a moment. When it did, he sat there transfixed.

Ty Roberts, the sheriff, passed the bank. Looking in through the window and seeing Oatman at his desk, he raised his hand in a friendly salute. Oatman saw him, but he was too preoccupied to respond. Finally, he said:

"I'm beginning to remember you. You're one of the three men who robbed this institution. It was you who shoved the gun in my face."

Rocky spread his hands in a deprecatory gesture.

"Why go into that, Mr. Oatman? You don't hear me accusing you of getting away with better than twenty-five thousand. All I'm saying is that there was a discrepancy. I'm not interested in who got it or where it went. Maybe you can explain. Maybe it would be mighty embarrassing if you were called on to try. I

33

know it would embarrass me if I had to explain how I happen to know so much about it."

Oatman glared at him in scornful silence for a moment.

"You've got brass, Jeanette—too much brass for your own good! You've overplayed your hand this time. I'll turn you over to the sheriff if it's the last thing I do on this earth."

Rocky shook his head, completely undisturbed.

"I'm sure you'll do nothing of sort—not when you've thought it over. You know my secret, Mr. Oatman, and I know yours. We'll do well to leave it that way."

"Who else knows it?" Oatman demanded tensely.

"No one."

"There were three—"

"Two of them are dead. No brains, Mr. Oatman. They tried a little job on their own and were killed. It makes everything airtight for us. We'll never have to worry about them."

Charlie Oatman thought long and hard.

"What's your price, Jeanette? How much do you want to clear out of Boulder City and never come back?"

"You don't get me at all, Mr. Oatman," Rocky protested, with a mild show of impatience. "I've got a few thousand; I'm not after your money. Nor am I interested in leaving town. I spent a lot of time thinking things out before I made a move. I figure I can do all right here."

"Not in the real estate and insurance business. You'll be lucky to make a living."

"After I get set, maybe I can branch out."

Oatman nodded. "That's what I'm afraid of." It was cool in the bank, but his thinning reddish hair was damp with perspiration.

"You needn't be afraid of that—not the way you mean it," Rocky told him. "I'll make myself a credit to Boulder City. The law will never have any occasion to put a finger on me. And not because I'm so honest all of a sudden. There's a better reason; I know the other way doesn't pay off."

Oatman had aged ten years in the past few minutes. He took out a handkerchief and mopped his face and polished his glasses. Desperate, his head throbbing so violently he could not think clearly, he could find no way to escape from his dilemma. He wasn't underestimating Rocky. Up to now the man had used a velvet paw. But the claws were there, concealed and ready to be used if he were defied.

The gun in the open drawer mocked Oatman with its nearness. He doubted that his trembling fingers could pick it up cleanly and use it quickly enough to count. Without doubt Rocky was armed and no novice with a gun. Then, too, killing him would leave some ugly questions to be answered.

Rocky followed his train of thought perfectly.

"I'm glad you see it that way, Mr. Oatman," he said quietly. "Neither one of us could afford anything like that."

He reached out and closed the drawer.

"Give me the same break I'm giving you," he went on. "That's all I want."

Oatman regarded him with a vast and bitter distrust.

"Be done with your fiendish cat and mouse game!"

he whipped out thinly. "You've got your price, and you expect me to pay it! Why sit there and tell me you're giving me a break?"

"I'll tell you why," said Rocky. "If a fellow walks into a bank with a gun in his fist, he's there to take whatever he can grab, and he doesn't intend to return it. There's no excuse for him unless he changes his ways. It's different with an honorable man who has done everything he could for his community. If things suddenly go wrong for him and he gets caught in a financial jam, maybe he takes a chance to save himself, figuring he can make good if he can buy a little time. Usually it works out all right. Sometimes it goes the other way. That doesn't make an honorable man a crook, in my eyes. After all, Mr. Oatman, what's twenty-five, thirty thousand dollars to you?" Rocky spread his hands eloquently. "You're a rich man. Let the market come back a little and the price of beef go up. Why, you'll be sitting pretty again. I'm sure you'll find some way of reimbursing the bonding company— and without anyone being the wiser. But that's your business."

Rocky was all steel now, his gray eyes cold and purposeful.

"I don't want to know what you do about it, but I can tell you that I don't propose ever to refer to it again. That's what I mean when I say give me the same break I'm giving you. I want you to take me as I am and forget the past."

They fenced with their eyes for a long moment and Oatman unconsciously moistened his parched lips with his tongue.

"Jeanette, you don't mean a word of it. You're too smooth and too hard for that. What you propose to do is grind me down—keep me under your heel. I won't know from one hour to the next where I stand. Whenever it pleases your purpose, you'll turn the screws. You'll enjoy seeing me squirm. If I don't dance to your tune, you'll threaten me with exposure and disgrace."

"No, Oatman," Rocky denied stoutly, "I'm too smart to risk anything like that. To put it bluntly, you've got as much on me as I have on you. I figure that's your guarantee and mine that neither of us will start rocking the boat."

Oatman shook his head hopelessly.

"You've got the whip hand on me from the start. Exposure and disgrace would mean little to you; I've got my family to think of—my wife and daughter—and my position in Boulder City. You've got something definite in mind, Jeanette. What is it? What do you want me to do for you?"

"I want you to set me in with the right people. I'll buy out Morrell. The bank controls a lot of insurance business through the mortgages it holds. You can shove it my way. Anybody who is anybody in Boulder City belongs to the Business Men's Club. When you get around to it, I'd appreciate it if you took me to one of the weekly luncheons and put me up for membership."

Oatman winced. Rocky's demands were modest, but he told himself this was only the beginning.

"All right," he muttered soberly, "I've got to knuckle under to you. But I'm warning you: watch your step carefully. There's a limit beyond which I won't go, no matter what it does to me."

As they sat talking, someone tapped on the window. It was Tony. She beckoned for her father to let her in. Oatman stifled a groan.

"This is my daughter," he snapped. "I'll have to ask you to leave, Jeanette."

"Certainly," Rocky agreed, though he intended to force an introduction if necessary. "We've finished our business. I'll open a modest account with the bank to-morrow. Some papers will have to be drawn up between Morrell and me. I'll need a lawyer. Can you suggest a good one?"

"Frank Grimwood is the attorney for the bank. His offices are across the street in the Oatman Building."

They walked to the door together. Tony was standing there when it was opened.

Oatman intended that Rocky should step out and be on his way. The situation grew more awkward by the second when he stood his ground. It forced the banker's hand.

"Tony, this is Mr. Jeanette; my daughter," he said. Rocky bowed.

"This is a pleasure, Miss Oatman."

Tony had a smile for him.

"Your first visit to Boulder City, Mr. Jeanette?"

"No—I've been here before," he said, with the slightest hesitation. "This time, I'm here to stay."

Tony glanced at her father for an explanation.

"Mr. Jeanette is taking over Carl Morrell's business," the latter explained.

"Then we'll be seeing each other often, Mr. Jeanette," said Tony. "Mr.—"

"William Jeanette. My friends call me Rocky."

"Rocky." Tony tried the sound of it on her lips. "After you get settled, you must come up to the house for dinner some evening."

An apoplectic hue swept over Oatman's face. Tony didn't notice; Rocky had her attention.

"That's kind of you," he said. He thanked her again, and, saying good afternoon, took his leave.

Tony's eyes followed him as he crossed the street.

"What an attractive man," she murmured. "He has a very engaging way about him, Father."

"Very!" Oatman muttered grimly.

5

"CHARLES, I SIMPLY CAN'T UNDERSTAND YOUR ATTI-
tude toward Mr. Jeanette," Celia Oatman said one
evening as she and her husband sat out on the porch
after dinner. They were alone at the time. "Tony and
I never mention his name but what you manage to let
us know you disapprove of him. It's not like you to be
two-faced about anything."

Oatman glanced up from his newspaper. The past
three weeks had been trying ones for him. He had held
himself in and thought he had handled the unbear-
able situation rather well.

"What do you mean by that, Ceel?" he inquired.

"Why, away from this house, you can't do enough
for William Jeanette. You sponsored him at the club
and have introduced him around among your friends
and business acquaintances. I don't believe it's any
secret that you are sending every bit of business you can
to him."

"I wouldn't worry about it," he advised rather

brusquely. "A stranger shows up in town who may be acceptable in a business way; that doesn't mean you have to take him into your home. He's been here for dinner two or three times already. I've noticed how you and Tony go out of your way to be nice to him. If Frank Grimwood is lucky enough to be asked up, he's treated to pot-luck with us. Not Jeanette; there has to be fussing and fixings."

"That's unfair," Mrs. Oatman protested. "You know how much I admire Frank. He's always welcome. When he first came to town, two years ago, I fussed, as you put it, for him. But you don't keep that up after you get to be old friends. I always say you never really know anyone until you can eat in the kitchen with them without feeling embarrassed."

"That's my point exactly," he observed. "We don't know anything about Jeanette. And you needn't ask me what I've got against him. I haven't anything against him. I just don't like to see you and Tony going out of your way to be so nice to him—pressing these invitations on him."

"He's being invited everywhere—the Woodruffs, the Bonfils, the Taylors." Celia Oatman smiled to herself. She thought she knew this husband of hers rather well. "I wonder, Charles, if you're not a bit jealous of him."

"Jealous?" Oatman's tone was crisp with amazement.

"Over that deal he made for the vacant corner lot next to the Bon Ton. I know you've had your eye on it for a long time. I remember you told me you were sure you could turn it over to Louie Abramson at a nice profit if you could get your hands on it."

"So I could have," Oatman admitted. "Jeanette made a nice thing out of it. He went down to Rawlins, caught Mrs. Chapin in the right mood and talked her into selling. I don't begrudge him his profit. Louie's going to build right away, a two-story brick to match the rest of the Bon Ton. That'll make Bridger Street look better; that vacant corner has always been an eyesore to me."

He turned back to his newspaper, or pretended to. It was his way of indicating that he had nothing further to say. He had known no peace of mind in weeks. Reading the *Mercury* had become a perfunctory chore that never claimed his whole attention even briefly, the unhappy position into which he had been maneuvered weighing so heavily on him that he had little interest in other people's troubles and pleasures.

The situation held a measure of bitter irony for him, too; the securities market had begun to recover and beef prices were climbing higher than anyone had reason to expect. Rocky's prediction was coming to pass; in a few weeks he would be back on solid ground, financially.

Charlie Oatman found little comfort in his returning prosperity; it came too late. Two months back, it would have made everything right for him. But no longer could money make him a free man; he was chained to Rocky. Making full restitution to the bonding company would not break those shackles. It would loosen their grip on him, however, and make it possible for him to fight back. But even that was denied him.

Oatman had given it a lot of thought. He had even considered ways as absurd as finding a sack of money that the bandits had dropped in their haste. It always brought him up against a stone wall: the State Bank Examiner had gone over the carefully doctored books and found nothing amiss. So had the auditors for the bonding company. Those figures had to stand now. They were his figures; question them, and the roof would fall in on him.

The whole situation was so fantastic that there were times when he tried to tell himself it couldn't be true; that it was only a cruel nightmare from which he would presently awaken. The strain he was under had begun to affect his health. But there was no one, his wife and daughter least of all, to whom he could unburden himself. Fearing and loathing Rocky, he had scrutinized every move the man made; though he was forced to acknowledge, however grudgingly, that, up to now, Rocky had conducted himself in an exemplary manner, it only served to deepen his conviction that, sooner or later, the crookedness and larceny that were in the self-confessed young blackleg would come to the surface.

Celia Oatman regarded her husband in silence, over the top of his newspaper. The change in him had been too marked of late to escape her notice. She had made several unsuccessful attempts to get to the bottom of it. Her first thought had been that it was something at the bank that was troubling him. He had scoffed at the suggestion.

"Charles, why don't you drop in and see Dr. Wingaard and let him look you over?" she said, without warning. Oatman brought his newspaper down promptly.

43

"What's the reason for that?" he demanded irritably. "There's nothing wrong with me. I don't need any of Wingaard's pills."

"There's something wrong with you," she insisted. "I can't imagine what it is. Is it possible you're worrying over Tony? I mean about her and Rocky Jeanette."

"Of course I'm worried!" he blurted out, exasperation getting the better of him. "I don't like it a little bit, I can tell you! She's getting entirely too thick with him to suit me. She knows she can paint; she doesn't need Jeanette to tell her so. But she seems to eat up everything he has to say. Tossing Charlie Russell's name at her, and a couple other Western painters who have hit the top, as though he was on intimate terms with them! Tony's always been so level-headed, you'd think she'd see through his cheap flattery . . . And what about Frank Grimwood? I understood she was in love with him."

Celia Oatman believed she at last had the answer to the riddle that had perplexed her for days, and there was a note of relief in her soft laughter.

"You are distressing yourself needlessly, Charles. There's nothing romantic about Tony's interest in Rocky. I know." Celia pressed her lips together firmly. She could be very positive when occasion required. "He's entertaining; he's been everywhere. Naturally, she enjoys his company. I'm glad she's found someone here who understands her viewpoint. Getting upset over anything as innocent as this is ridiculous. Certainly Frank Grimwood doesn't object.

44

If he felt he was in any danger of playing second fiddle to Rocky, they wouldn't be so friendly."

"Hunh!" was Oatman's caustic comment. "I hope you're right!" Not trying to hide his annoyance, he got up and put on his hat. "I'm going downtown for a few minutes."

There was the usual Saturday night excitement along Bridger Street. All the stores were open and most of them busy, catering to the needs of men and women who had driven in from the nearby ranches. The saloons, especially the popular Maverick, a cowboy stronghold, were crowded.

Four punchers, their mood hilarious, came down the sidewalk, spur chains jangling, and turned into the Maverick. Oatman recognized them for part of Joe Evans' crew. Joe had two carloads of feeders down in the Wyoming & Western yard. Obviously, these men were in town to drive the cattle out to the Circle E on faraway Joe Creek.

Oatman glanced up at the windows of Frank Grimwood's offices and found them dark. At the hotel, he bought a cigar and had a look around the lobby, half expecting to find Rocky and Frank there. It had got so that if you saw one you usually saw the other. But not tonight.

"They're all out to the lake, I suppose," he thought.

It was a safe surmise, for there was an informal dance every Saturday night at what Boulder City always referred to as the "Club." Rocky wasn't a member as yet, but he was often there, usually as Grimwood's guest.

He found the lake an enjoyable spot. The old

45

Heneker ranch house, that had stood there for years, remained as it had been, save for the addition of a long veranda on the side of the house facing the water. A grove of cottonwoods and cedars provided more greenery than could be found anywhere else short of the upper reaches of the Dry Creek Mountains. There were bathing, boating and some fishing, which was a pleasant escape from the hot, dry summers that beat down mercilessly on Boulder City.

Tony had driven out this evening with Frank and Rocky. They had become a familiar threesome at the lake. Without any help from her, several town girls had tried unsuccessfully to make it a foursome. Rocky hadn't given them any encouragement, either. With ingratiating diplomacy, however, he had avoided turning his admirers into enemies. Furthermore, he wasn't permitting his interest in Tony to get out of hand. She wasn't making it easy for him. In his conceit, he added up little things that made him believe he could take her away from Grimwood. He knew Frank was devoted to her. It was not because he had become genuinely fond of the young lawyer that he held off; Grimwood could help him to get on and that came first with Rocky.

He wasn't underestimating Frank Grimwood, with his plain face and quiet, self-effacing manner, the least bit; beneath the mild surface, Rocky saw a man of stern, fighting character who wasn't likely to be betrayed by his emotions nor turned aside from any goal he set for himself. There were characteristics of great virtue in Rocky's eyes. He was convinced that he himself was cut along those lines. Accordingly, he respected Grimwood and never forgot to be careful with him.

Dancing with Tony, Rocky caught a glimpse of Grimwood standing in the veranda doorway, an amused smile on his face. Rocky swung that way and asked him if he wanted to cut in.

"No," Frank answered. "Buck's going too strong for me right now. I'll wait till he cools off a bit."

The music, piano and violin, left a lot to be desired. Whenever he could get in from the ranch of a Saturday night, Buck Neville gave the two musicians a dubious assist with his cornet. Buck was present this evening, enjoying himself immensely, embellishing his efforts with uncertain frills and flourishes and taking no notice whatever of the sour notes in between. Whatever his playing lacked in musical accomplishment, it had vim and vigor, which was to be expected of a man who thought nothing of riding thirty miles, after a long day's work in the saddle, to toot a horn at a dance.

Rocky and Tony danced away.

"You're very pretty tonight, Tony," he murmured.

"Thank you," she said, acknowledging the compliment with a pleased smile. "Nothing special. I'm beginning to feel thoroughly rested for the first time since I got back . . . I understand you and Frank are pulling out at daylight for the desert."

Rocky nodded.

"You'll enjoy it if the wind doesn't kick up. I've been over parts of the Blue Rock many times. I love its moods. Perhaps that's why I always find it a bit scary . . . Frank's going to show you what he's found out there, of course."

"Yeh." Rocky grinned. "He says he'll convince me that there's oil there."

47

"Do you know anything about oil?"

"Not a thing. No one seems to think Frank knows anything about it, either. But I don't know why there shouldn't be oil in Wyoming. Come up with a new idea, or try to do something different, and the usual run of people will say it's nonsense."

Tony nodded.

"Don't I know? When I said I was going to paint, everyone said I was crazy. The only encouragement I got was from Mom. It used to shock Father almost to death to have me walk into the bank in Levis and cotton shirt to tell him I was going out on the range alone for a day or two with my easel. To this day Joe Evans doesn't think it seemly for me to be hanging around cow camps and Indian Reservations. But I guess he's gradually coming around to thinking I may amount to something. I caught him in the bank yesterday, sitting there studying that painting of mine. He had a faraway look in his eyes, as though it had rolled back the years for him."

Rocky's mood was suddenly sober.

"You're having a good time, Tony—doing what you want to do. A person can make a mistake or two but if he believes in himself that won't stop him; he can get about what he wants out of life."

She looked up at him, wondering what lay behind his words. His gray eyes were unreadable. In his face, however, she found something that she had never seen there before. It was as though something deep within him had momentarily come to the surface, touching him with a vague and obscure regret.

48

Tony felt the tug of it. She didn't ask herself why. Rocky smiled then and the moment was gone.

"Frank should know something about oil," she said quickly, looking away. "His father was an oil man back in Wood County, Ohio. Frank worked in the field with him every summer while he was going through law school. He's studied geology and petrology, so he isn't going altogether by guess or by gosh . . . I don't suppose I'm telling you anything you don't already know."

"No," Rocky admitted. "He's talked my arm off."

"Don't discourage him, Rocky." It was her turn to be serious. "Frank's the salt of the earth. He's very fond of you."

After an encore, they walked out on the veranda and sat down at a table with Frank. They had been there only a moment or two, when the latter waved to two late comers.

"Who is it, Frank?" Tony inquired.

"Why, it's Rita Warren and the judge! I didn't know she was back. She must have got in this evening."

He was pleasantly excited, and so was Tony.

"Ask them to come over and sit down with us," she urged. "You'll like Rita; she's always fun," she added in an aside to Rocky.

Frank brought Mrs. Warren and Judge Bonfils to the table. Rocky was acquainted with the judge. There were four Bonfils brothers in Boulder City, and all had done well. Sam, Lee and Bert Bonfils owned the Bonfils Cattle Company and an imposing string of ranches. Though he was nearing fifty, Judge Ira, a confirmed

49

bachelor, was the youngest, and, as Rocky was to learn, he was Rita Warren's adviser and close friend.

"I got in on the 8:02," Rita explained. "The Judge was at the depot to meet me. He suggested that I stay at the hotel tonight and that we come out to the lake for an hour or two, so here we are . . . You are visiting in Boulder City, Mr. Jeanette?"

"No," Grimwood answered for Rocky with a laugh, "he's permanent and on his way to becoming one of our first citizens."

He filled in the details.

"Well!" Rita exclaimed. She sounded pleased. "I hope we'll be seeing you at the ranch, Mr. Jeanette. You'll always find the latchstring out for you."

Tony, who knew Rita well, thought she was being unduly friendly and didn't like it. Rocky saw her lips tighten momentarily and read her thought. He was finding Rita far too interesting to be concerned about anything else for the moment. She had a dark, sultry beauty that reflected her California-Spanish ancestry and a worldly self-assurance that he found intoxicating. He surmised that she was about his own age, half-a-dozen years older than Tony.

"Better than I expected," she answered, when Grimwood asked how she had done on the Coast. "I've shipped my string to Denver for the September Meeting. I'll be home about ten days before I go down."

"I suppose you'll go on to San Antonio and Juarez?" Bonfils remarked.

"Not Juarez." Rita shook her head in a very definite no. "I'll never start a horse there again. I don't expect judges to see things my way always, but when one of my boys is fouled and then goes on to win, only to be charged with the offense and have the race taken away from him, I refuse to turn the other cheek. I have Hannibal entered in the Texas Handicap and another entry or two at San Antonio. That'll wind things up for me until I ship to New Orleans this winter. But enough about me. What are you working on, Tony?"

"I haven't been doing a thing," Tony answered carelessly. The edge had been taken off the evening for her, though she refused to admit it.

"Too many diversions?" was Rita's probing query, accompanied by a glance that included Rocky.

"In Boulder City?" Tony meant her laughter to be only incredulous but it had a faint sting.

Rocky smiled to himself, thinking he understood what lay behind this feminine dueling, and admiring the ease with which Rita had turned the conversation away from herself.

"I'm going out to the Taylors' on Monday for a few days," Tony said, making a sudden decision. "I'll stay at the ranch but spend my time up in that wild horse country to the north. I know what I want to do. I always have to see a picture before I attempt it."

"I'll wager it tells a story," the Judge declared. "Your paintings always do, Tony. What's this one going to be about?"

"A cow pony that's broken away from a ranch and joined the wild bunch. He's left his cowboy pardner behind. There's a deep affection between them. That's what I've got to put over—their love for each other."

"And?" Grimwood urged, as she broke off. "Don't leave us up in the air that way, Tony."

"Well," she continued, "this cowpuncher goes trailing the pony and finds him out on the alkali flats with the broom-tails. He gets close enough to call to him. The wild ones make a run for it, but that familiar voice holds the pony. The man is walking toward the horse, coiled rope in his hand. In the background, the wild ones are running hard, but the leader of the band has stopped and is looking back inquiringly at the backslider from freedom. The pony glances that way. He has to decide between his natural desire to run free with his own kind and his love for the man, and he doesn't know what to do. I'm going to call it The Cross Pull."

"The Cross Pull—that's good," Rocky observed, with unexplained gravity. "Something pulling you one way and something else pulling you the other." He wasn't thinking about horses. "You put all that in a picture, Tony, and you'll have something."

6

WHEN GRIMWOOD ARRIVED AT THE HOTEL AT FOUR the next morning, with a saddled horse for Rocky, he found the latter waiting.

"I swear you look like a dude in those togs," he declared laughingly. "Everything brand new from boots to hat."

"And they feel like it," Rocky told him. "I didn't have any range clothes; I had to outfit myself . . . This is a good-looking bronc you've got for me."

"One of the sheriff's horses. Ty keeps a good string."

Rocky swung up easily.

"No need to ask if you can ride," Grimwood observed. "The way you climbed into that saddle is the tip-off."

"I've done a little riding," said Rocky, and immediately changed the subject. "What about breakfast? There doesn't seem to be anything open."

"There's an all-night Chink restaurant down by the

depot that isn't too bad. I've got some grub for this noon and Rita's invited us to stop there for supper on our way back this evening. Remember?"

Rocky nodded. It was an invitation he had promptly accepted.

A quick breakfast, and they were on their way. The sun was just getting up.

"Prettiest time of the day in this Western country," said Rocky, as they began to put Boulder City behind them. To the north, the Dry Creek Mountains appeared to have the color and texture of puffs of pink and lavender cotton. The air was redolent with the tang of sage brush.

"It is," Grimwood agreed. "Tony's got me out early enough on two or three occasions to reach the crest of Round Butte in time to witness the whole show." He indicated Round Butte, five miles to the east, with a jerk of his head. "The sunrise takes your breath away, when you're up there."

"And it's different every morning," remarked Rocky, his guard down. "You might not think it, but that's so; the colors are never quite the same. It gets to a man."

Grimwood regarded him with a puzzled light in his eyes. Rocky caught him shaking his head and was wary at once.

"What is it?" he asked, with deceiving carelessness.

Grimwood chuckled.

"I swear, you knock me off my pins ever so often by saying something that I'd never expect to hear from a city-bred stranger to Wyoming . . . You sure you're a tenderfoot?" he added facetiously.

"I'm beginning to wonder," was Rocky's bantering

response. He knew he had slipped up. He was too wise to walk away from it without covering himself. The truth seemed to be the best and handiest weapon. "I've been around some. I don't know where you get that city-bred stuff; western Missouri was my home range, and when I pulled away from the town where I was born it was still just a wide spot in the road. The only time anyone ever heard anything about that neck of the woods was when Frank and Jesse James were on the loose."

"Thank God you didn't take a leaf out of their book," said Grimwood. "You wouldn't be selling insurance in Boulder City today if you had."

Rocky shrugged and said, "You never can tell about things like that . . . Let's push these broncs a little, Frank. We got a long way to go, and it's going to be hot later."

The Spanish Ranch was not yet astir when they passed. This was the first time Rocky had seen it at close range. It was obvious at a glance that money had been poured into it with a lavish hand. The main house was a rambling structure of stone and stucco, with a tile roof. Between it and the cluster of buildings around the stable and barns stood an old, comfortable-looking two-story frame house.

"That's the old Warren ranch house that stood here when this was a cow ranch," Grimwood explained. "That was before old Mark Warren, Ted's father, pulled up stakes and went to Montana and made a million dollars in copper. It's an attractive-looking house today. A lot of work's been done on it. I've heard Rita say that when she first saw it, it was just a wooden box with a roof on it. Jim Fitzpatrick, her trainer, and his family live there. He's had the Warren horses from the beginning. Those bungalows down by the stables are for the riders and exercise boys and the crew that works the ranch."

"Took money to do all that," said Rocky.

"Rita has plenty left." It answered Rocky's un-asked question. "She doesn't throw it away like Ted did. He was a crazy man with money."

"What happened to him? An accident?"

"Yeh, hunting accident. Nobody knows exactly what occurred. He was up in the Tetons, hunting elk, with a couple friends from the East. He didn't come into camp one evening. The guide found him next morning, shot through the head. That was a few months after I landed in Boulder City. It was the general opinion that Rita was well rid of him; he'd been living on whisky for a year or more."

Overnight Rocky had canvassed his mind regarding Rita Warren. She was not only tailored to his liking but she could be the brake that would stop him from getting over his head with Tony Oatman.

He thought it over again this morning, as Grimwood and he skirted the eastern fringe of the Slate Hills. Stripped of all else, attaching himself to Rita held a promise of safety for him, and not only because it would help him to maintain the status quo with Tony and Grimwood.

"She's no kid," he mused. "In the back of her head, she'll question everything I do. That'll make me care-ful on her account as well as my own. I might be sucker enough to toss away the chance I've got in this town if I didn't have somebody to slow me up."

The country began to change soon after they struck away from the hills. By nine o'clock, they had open desert ahead of them.

"The place we're heading for is called Mustard Valley," Grimwood turned in his saddle to remark. "Just sand, alkali flats and a little dwarf sage. There's a big dry wash down the middle of it. I don't know why they call it a valley. It's really a big desert coulée —a mile-wide depression surrounded by ragged hills that were leveled off by glacial action. Look ahead, far down on the horizon, and you can see the flat-tops I mean . . . You know that rock formations have been classified into age groups."

Rocky nodded but didn't appear too sure.

"You find crude petroleum only in the higher strata, never in metamorphic or crystalline formations. All the other geological systems have produced it. Competent authorities say that if oil is found in this part of the United States it will be in the cretaceous strata. That's what we've got here."

He grinned as he saw the puzzled look on Rocky's face.

"Does all that scare you?" he queried.

"Sounds pretty bad, Frank."

"Well, don't worry; I won't snow you under with scientific junk. I'll convince you without going into that."

Another hour's riding brought them to the barrier reef of slashed-off hills, or buttes, that encircled Mustard Valley. Grimwood pulled up when they had the valley spread out below them.

"There's my oil-field; Mustard Valley."

"And a tough-looking spot she is!" Rocky declared with bitter emphasis. "Doesn't look as though even a coyote could scratch a living down there."

"It's no bower of roses," Grimwood admitted. "Most—maybe all—of the Blue Rock Desert was under water at one time. It must have been a big salt lake. I've found traces of a shore line in these hills and away over in the Dry Creek Mountains. No trick to find salt-water fossils."

"And that's good?"

"Well, it ain't bad, Rocky. There're two or three schools of thought on the origin of petroleum. The graybeards used to think it was an inorganic substance, distilled from coal under great pressure. The majority opinion today is that it's the result of the decomposition of marine organisms, animal and vegetable. But let's get down there and poke around a little. I want to give you something more substantial than theory."

They picked their way down and ground-tied the ponies. Rocky looked around, trying to locate the wide dry wash Grimwood had mentioned. Its banks were so shallow, in relation to the rest of the depression that he had to ask Frank to point it out to him.

"I can see it now," Rocky said. "It hasn't carried any water to speak of in a good many years. A little, I suppose, in the spring, when the snow's going off."

Grimwood agreed with him.

"Its only value to me has been to indicate the direction of the natural drainage and the surface flow in centuries past. Following that line, it wasn't difficult to find the lowest point in the depression. I knew if there was any oil seepage—and I'd been told there was —it would be there."

"Was there?" Rocky was beginning to be interested.

"I'll say there was. Chances are you never heard anyone mention Matt Bell. He passed away last winter. He was an old-time prospector. There wasn't much about the Blue Rock he didn't know. It was Matt who first got me interested in looking for oil out here. He swore he had often seen a little pool of black gumbo that smelled like tar, in Mustard Valley. But you have a look, Rocky, and see what you make of it. I cached a testing stick by this sandstone outcropping. I'll get it, and we'll go on."

He dug out of the sand a stick the size and shape of a billiard cue. Fitted to the small end was a pointed iron shoe.

They had only a few hundred yards to go. Rocky led the way. He noticed numerous footprints in the sand and pointed them out to Grimwood.

"Have you had company in here, Frank?"

"No, they're mine. I've been looking them over. No one been here since I was in last."

Rocky caught the tangy smell of coal tar a few seconds before he caught sight of the pool, which was only four and a half to five feet wide and very shallow. A gummy, iridescent film covered it.

"You mean to tell me that's crude oil?" he asked, the last trace of boredom gone.

"It's water. Only that film floating on the surface is oil, and I'll prove to you that it *is* oil and not iron oxide or some similar substance. Here, take the stick and stir it around in the pool till you've broken up the film. Then watch it reunite."

Rocky did as directed. The iridescent film separated for a split second and then showed an unbroken surface.

"If that slick was due to an iron oxide, you'd be able to break it up into little flakes that you could move around," Grimwood told him. "Pull your stick out now and look at the iron shoe. You'll see drops of water adhering to it like you will on any greasy or fatty substance."

Rocky repeated the test a number of times and always got the same result.

"I'm a greenhorn about this, but you're making me see it your way," he declared, unmistakably impressed and not trying to conceal the fact. "You may have your fingers on a million dollars, Frank!"

Grimwood shook his head skeptically.

"I don't doubt but what there're many millions here for someone. I'm afraid it's as far away as the moon for me. It's going to cost a small fortune to put down a test well—twice as much as it would cost back in Ohio or Pennsylvania, where wells are being put down every day. You couldn't raise the money in Boulder City. Money for a ranch, or a gold mine, but not for an oil well. Go to Charlie Oatman or Hank Taylor or the Bonfils bunch and they'd walk away from you as though you had the smallpox."

"Maybe something can be done about that." Rocky spoke with a mysterious confidence. "We can talk about it later. You're sure there's oil here, Frank?"

"As sure as I could be about anything."

"Then tell me this—remember I'm an absolute greenhorn—if this little pool has been here for years, and its seepage, why hasn't it got any bigger?"

"There's porous sandstone just below the surface. You can see the outcroppings. But go down any place and you'll strike it in a few feet. The oil has been drifting across it. I've chipped off pieces all around here and given them the so-called water test. You place the piece of rock in a pan of water and expose it to the sun. If there's oil in it, iridescent colors will appear on the surface almost at once. I've never failed to get them. I'll get a pick and make a fresh fracture for you; we can spare enough water for the test."

The fragment he chipped off was darker than sandstone usually is, indicating that it was impregnated with oil. Placed in water, it immediately gave off streaks of rainbow-like colors.

"My dad used to be fond of saying that an oil deposit wasn't unlike a leaky pot with a good strong lid," said Grimwood. "What he meant was that you need a stratum of porous rock for your reservoir and an impervious rock lid to hold the oil there. If you get a little seepage like this it's because of the gas pressure behind it. I could tell you a lot about tectonic arches and the part structural conditions play and how water and oil divide, owing to the difference in their density, with the oil filling the anticlines and water the synclines, but I'd get so involved you'd yell murder."

"You don't have to say any more." Rocky's imagination had caught fire and he was deadly serious now. "I'm convinced you've got something. It's a good thing

no one in town is taking you seriously, or some smart
gent would be cutting under you."

Grimwood laughed at the suggestion, and said, "No
danger of that."

"Don't be too sure," Rocky said thinly. "You
wouldn't be the first party who'd talked himself out of
a fortune."

He turned his back on a whirling spiral of dust and
watched it go dancing up the wash.

"Let's move into the base of that hill and try to find
some shade and get out of this dust. It's time to eat,
anyhow."

"Okay," Grimwood agreed. "I'll get my pack. You
pick up a little dead sage for a fire and we'll boil some
coffee."

Nooning under an overhanging cliff proved to be
a pleasant interlude. This was the first time in several
months that Rocky had been out in the open. It was
good to have the pungent aroma of burning sage biting
his nostrils again. Grimwood heated a panful of beans
and fried some bacon.

They talked while they ate. Afterwards, Rocky was
thoughtful as he smoked. He had journeyed into the
desert with Grimwood with no other purpose in mind
than to humor him and enjoy the day. Had it occurred
to him, he would have ridiculed the thought that he
was to become seriously interested in a wildcat oil pros-
pect. That was all changed now; his eyes had been
opened and he saw an opportunity beckoning to him
that was so rich that it dwarfed his modest business
into insignificance. If the optimism he expressed
sounded lukewarm, it was intentional, for he was in the

throes of asking himself why he shouldn't go it alone. Why bother with Grimwood? He could deal Frank out and have it all to himself.

Such a course appealed to his rapacious instincts. In the past, that had been the compelling consideration with him. Strangely, he hesitated about embracing it now. He couldn't understand why he questioned it. It could have been conscience, or the awakening of some dormant scruple of honesty.

That didn't occur to him as he sat there trying to reach a decision and only half listening to Grimwood, who was talking about his youthful days in Ohio. Rocky found his answer by devious reasoning and had it all settled in his mind before he realized it. He'd play fair with Frank Grimwood. That was the sensible thing to do; he'd need Frank. If other, and less selfish, reasons impelled him, he refused to recognize them.

Staring out across the wastes of Mustard Valley and beyond, Rocky conjured up a picture of a forest of oil derricks and toiling men.

"Can you imagine the changes a producing oil field will make around here?" he mused. "It'll change everything. Boulder City will be a town of fifty thousand in a year or two."

"I've dreamed about it," Grimwood acknowledged.

"Suppose you stop dreaming and do something." Rocky's feigned detachment had fled. "Who owns this land?"

"It's state land."

"Can it be purchased?"

"Sure, and for a song."

"With all mineral rights?"

"Naturally."

"Then go ahead and buy five hundred acres."

"Wait a minute!" Grimwood protested. "I'm a young lawyer, just getting started. I haven't any such amount of loose money laying around."

"I'll put up the dough," said Rocky.

Grimwood gazed at him with mingled surprise and incredulity. "I didn't bring you out here to sell you a bill of goods, Rocky . . . You can't mean you're ready to throw in with me."

"You got a pardner," Rocky answered. "Buy this land, and keep what you're doing under your hat till we've got the deed. We're in this fifty-fifty. It'll be up to me to raise the money for the well. I'll get it somewhere. How much is it going to take?"

"Thirty, thirty-five, maybe fifty thousand dollars. You can't name a figure and keep it. What oil there is here can't be too deep. Twenty-seven hundred to three thousand feet. But a contractor may lose a string of tools and have to spend weeks fishing for them. If he can't get them out, he'll have to begin all over."

The figure was higher than Rocky had expected, to say nothing of being surrounded with uncertainties. In his ignorance, he had believed that uncertainty in drilling an oil well was restricted to whether or not you struck oil.

Grimwood saw other difficulties that would have to be overcome in putting down a test well in a new field.

"Timbers for a seventy-foot derrick will have to be freighted out. That goes for casing, tools, boiler and the rest of the rig. There isn't any road. Most of the way is level desert that won't give a heavy freighting outfit any trouble. One or two places will take some work. I don't know of any water nearer than the Spanish Ranch, and water will be needed for the boiler and the crew. We'll have to keep a water-wagon on the go every day. There'll be the matter of getting grub out here, too, and feed for the teams."

Grimwood saw Rocky's frown deepen.

"We'd better be realistic about these things and realize what we'll be up against," he pointed out.

"Sure," Rocky muttered. "You haven't mentioned anything that figures to stop us. How about the drilling? Will you have any trouble getting someone to come out to Wyoming to handle the job?"

"I won't have any trouble finding a contractor, but we'll have to pay him his price. In an established field, ninety cents to a dollar a foot is the average rate. We can't expect to get it done for anything like that. The contractor will find the tools and be responsible for accidents. It'll be up to us to build the derrick and supply the rig."

"Does the contractor have his own men?"

"He usually has his own crew—two drillers and a couple tool-dressers. That'll be the best deal for us. If we go through with it, I'll have to take a trip back East to make the arrangements."

"Don't worry; we'll go through with it," Rocky said flatly. "You draw up some papers tomorrow that'll cover the deal between us, and then you get busy seeing what you can do about buying this land."

Grimwood started to nod approvingly, checked himself abruptly, and was suddenly enormously sober.

"What's the matter?" Rocky demanded, a bit

nettled and not concealing the fact. "Anything wrong with that?"

"No, I was just thinking, Rocky. You intend to raise the money locally?"

"Sure!"

Grimwood's mouth tightened perceptibly.

"If the well comes in dry, we'll have to leave town, Rocky. There wouldn't be anything left for us in Boulder City. It's something to think about."

"I've thought about it," was the flinty response. "I know you're on the level. That's good enough for me. If this thing backfires and somebody has to leave town, it won't be you."

7

ROCKY AND GRIMWOOD HAD TALKED THEMSELVES OUT
by the time they left Mustard Valley. With the west-
ering sun in their eyes, they turned back over the way
they had come, exchanging only an occasional word and
leaving it to the horses to make the pace.

They were supposed to be examining the terrain with
the idea of finding a feasible route for a makeshift
road. Grimwood gave it his complete attention, and
such conversation as ensued between them was confined
to the subject. Rocky's frowning engrossment was
genuine enough, but it was not wholly concerned with
finding a road; he was beginning to wonder if he hadn't
been a little rash in committing himself so unreservedly
to the oil well venture. It was not his way, as a rule, to
back and fill about anything, and yet the thought kept
returning to him that he was running counter to his
sworn determination to play every card cautiously.
What he was doing now was to put all his eggs in one
basket, and it was a basket with a very weak handle.

If he hit the jack-pot, the rewards would be great. But that was a very large if.

"It'll take a couple weeks to make the deal for the land," he thought. "I can't back out of that, but even if I'm stuck for it, I'll have a little time to think things over before I go any further."

Up ahead, Grimwood had reined in.

"This is one of the bad spots I had in mind, Rocky. The sand's so deep I don't believe a heavy freighter could get through even if we put down two or three feet of sagebrush. The brush would be ground out of sight a day or two after we got it laid."

Rocky stood up in his stirrups to see better and surveyed the sand, trying to find a route around it. It stretched away on either hand as far as he could see.

"There's a lot of it," he said. "It looks even worse off to the north. Suppose we swing the other way and see what we can find."

They rode for more than a mile before they found good going. They continued on to the southwest, instead of turning back to the course they had taken that morning. They encountered several more stretches of bad sand but were able to get around them rather easily. A mean dry wash, narrow and deep, presented a more formidable obstacle.

"No laughing this off," Rocky commented. "Looks like it runs through here for a couple miles."

They moved along it, first in one direction and then in the other, without finding a favorable crossing.

"One spot is as bad as another," said Grimwood. "This wash isn't the result of a cloudburst; it carries a heavy run-off every spring, by the looks of it. The way to lick it is to put in a good-sized culvert and then break down the banks for fill. We're not more than five miles from the Slate Hills now. There's good hard surface all the way around them to the county road that we came over this morning, when we passed the Spanish Ranch. So maybe this is the only real headache we'll have to worry about."

Rocky nodded and said, "I hope you're right. We can put these broncs across. Suppose we do and be on our way. It's getting late."

Rita stepped out on the veranda and waved a greeting, when they rode up to the house. She was fresh and lovely, which Rocky and Grimwood, in their dusty condition, doubly appreciated. Knowing they would be in rough range clothes, and wanting them to be at ease, she had dressed simply, tweed skirt and white silk blouse, open at the neck to reveal the symmetry of her throat.

Another woman might not have thought of it, but this bit of feminine wisdom, trifling in itself, was characteristic of Rita and helped to explain her success with men.

"I'm glad to see the two of you," she said, glancing approvingly at Rocky. "I like you in that rig. The only thing that's missing is a gun-belt and .45." She turned to Grimwood for corroboration. "He looks like an honest-to-goodness cow dog, doesn't he, Frank?"

Grimwood's eyes kindled with a merry twinkle. "I've been telling him he's got a lot of savvy for a tenderfoot."

69

Rocky joined in on the laughter at his expense.

"Kid me if you want to," he told them, his bantering tone all innocence. "Maybe I could give a pretty good account of myself at that—if the chips were down and there was gunsmoke at the end of it."

"I bet you could!" Rita agreed, mimicking him perfectly. "You boys use the room at the end of the hall; I know you want to freshen up a bit."

They showered and scrubbed, and as Rocky ran a comb through his hair, he gazed at his reflection in the mirror with a keen appreciation of his good fortune. Once again he could tell himself that he was doing all right; that he hadn't made any mistake in returning to Boulder City.

On their way out to join Rita on the screened veranda, Rocky had a peek at the richly appointed dining room. The spacious living room had the same quiet luxury. Stranger though he was to refinement and good taste in such matters, he recognized them.

"I know you'll have a drink," Rita told them. "Posie will be out in a moment with the wagon."

They were just comfortably seated, when an aged Negro in white coat appeared with a rubber-tired cart that held ice and glasses and an array of liquor. Grimwood greeted him familiarly.

"Posie, this is Mr. Jeanette," Rita announced. "I'm hoping we'll be seeing him frequently."

Posie bowed and said, "The Spanish Ranch is a mighty pleasant spot, Mistah Jeanette, when Missy is to home . . . Yas, suh!" he added, wagging his head.

Rocky found the liquor excellent. The appetizing odors reaching him from the direction of the kitchen told him the food would be just as good. To call this gracious establishment, with its good living, a ranch house was shooting wide of the mark, he told himself. It was unlike any ranch house he had ever known. Its architecture might be on the Spanish side, but there was something here that smacked of the Blue Grass region of Kentucky.

Grimwood and Rocky had foreseen that there would be some talk of oil and their day on the Blue Rock. They had agreed that, for the present, the only thing they wanted to hold back was their decision to buy the land.

"I'm all ears to hear what you found," said Rita. Heretofore, she had never encouraged Frank to expound the subject. This evening, however, her tone suggested a lively interest in it. "I'm not asking you, Frank; I know you see gushers spouting all over the Blue Rock . . . How did it strike you, Mr. Jeanette?"

"I was favorably impressed," Rocky replied. "Of course, I had to look at it through Frank's eyes; all I know about an oil well is that it looks like a windmill without a wheel. In anything like this, I figure it's the man you've got to put your confidence in; if you're sure he's right, go ahead. If I had forty to fifty thousand dollars to spare, I'd take a gamble."

"I must say you sound enthusiastic," Rita declared. "With an endorsement like that, Frank, we may have to take you seriously, after all. I used to think you were just amusing yourself, running off into the desert to pick up shells and old bones and what not, every time you got the chance. Do the two of you actually mean to tell me there may be oil in the Blue Rock?"

Presented with such an opening, Grimwood could not resist making the most of it. Warming to his subject, he argued that there was oil in the Blue Rock just waiting for man to bring it to the surface. The known facts, all the visible evidence, said so, and he presented scientific logic to back it up. It was much the same argument that had won Rocky over. When Grimwood wanted to drive home a point, he turned to his silent partner for verification.

Rocky didn't hesitate to confirm the statements that were referred to him. He felt he could do so honestly. But that was not all that was in his mind, for though Frank had no ulterior purpose in trying to convince Rita, she was wealthy, and Rocky wasn't losing sight of the fact. If he went through with the deal, money would be needed. How better to start the ball rolling than to induce Rita Warren, with her prestige, to purchase a block of stock?

They were still on the subject, when Posie came out to announce that dinner was served.

Rocky, as he was so fond of saying, had been around. At one time or another, he had enjoyed the epicurean delights of such famous, though scattered, establishments as Antoine's in New Orleans, The Brown Palace in Denver and Davenport's in Spokane, and it was one of his vanities that he considered himself an excellent judge of fine food. He had looked forward to a good dinner, and Rita's Louisiana-born cook exceeded his fondest expectations. He pronounced the beef and kidney pie, with its flaky brown crust, the best he had ever eaten. He found the squash soufflé and corn pudding no less delectable.

"Crissy is one of my great treasures," Rita confessed. "She was raised on a plantation in Plaquemines Parish, in Louisiana, and literally grew up in a kitchen. When we engaged Mr. Fitzpatrick to take charge of our horses, he brought two colored boys with him. They were Crissy's sons. A year or so later, we were in New Orleans for the Fair Grounds Meeting. The boys went to work on Crissy and finally induced her to brave Wyoming. I'm sure nothing else would have done it."

"Press and Jonah are good boys," said Grimwood. "They've always behaved themselves. Press told me once that he and his brother had been in the racing game as far back as he could remember. It's no wonder they have a way with horses."

"It's all they know," said Rita. "As Mr. Fitz says, they're worth all the rest of the boys rolled together." She turned to Rocky. "Crissy's relatives are becoming something of a problem for me. About every six months, it seems, another one of her numerous nephews or grandsons shows up and I have to take him on to keep her happy. I'm beginning to wonder where it's going to end."

The conversation began to take a lighter turn, as they dined leisurely. Before they left the table, it was Rita and Rocky, when the two of them addressed each other.

"I'd like to show you over the place, Rocky," she said. "We can do that the next time you come. I've got some likely looking colts, most of them Hamilcar's get. He's a grand sire. You don't have to look any further than Hannibal for proof of that."

After dinner, Posie served them coffee on the veranda. Rita joined her guests in smoking a cigarette. In that day women—good women, and especially those in Wyoming—didn't smoke. She ignored that inhibition and made an alluring and effective weapon of it.

The horses Rocky and Grimwood had left at the rack had been taken down to the barns and fed. When it came time to leave, Rita said she would have the animals brought up.

"Don't bother," Grimwood told her. "I'll go down. I'd like to stop in and say hello to Mr. Fitz."

On the ranch, Jim Fitzpatrick was seldom referred to or addressed as other than Mr. Fitz.

Grimwood's going gave Rocky and Rita a minute alone.

"I don't know when I've enjoyed myself so much," he told her. "It's been a very pleasant evening."

"Don't let it be the last," she murmured. "You know the way now. Some time, I'm going to have you tell me why you decided to cast your lot in Boulder City."

Rocky grinned.

"I'll tell you now. I was in Denver, looking around for something to try my hand at. I didn't know which way to jump. I happened to pick up a week-old copy of the *Mercury*—I was getting ready to toss it aside, when I read that you were shipping your horses to California. I bought a racing sheet and saw that Hannibal was starting that afternoon at Emoryville. I put ten dollars on him to win. If he came in, I figured it would be the hunch I'd been looking for and I'd head for Boulder City. You know the rest. I've always been glad I came, but never so glad as right now. Knowing you makes it perfect."

"That's a very pretty compliment, Rocky. I appreciate it." Rita's smile was warm and inviting. "It's going to be nice having you around." She looked away and grew thoughtful. "Why don't you get behind this proposition of Frank's? It's a gamble, but it sounds good to me. You could give it the push that would put it over. Left to himself, he won't do anything with it."

"What do you mean?" Rocky asked, though he understood her perfectly.

"Promote it. Organize a stock company and sell shares. I'm used to taking chances; I'll come in for a thousand or two."

"I've given it some thought," Rocky acknowledged. "But you know how such things kick back on you, especially in a small town, if your deal turns out to be a dud. You can't take money from your neighbors and expect them to forgive you if they lose. It would be my finish. I'm speaking confidentially; I wouldn't care to have Frank, or anyone else, hear what I'm saying."

"I understand," said Rita. "I'm speaking in confidence to you, too. It would be easy to overstep yourself and promise too much. But you needn't make that mistake. Sell it as an outright gamble; don't promise anything. If you strike oil, the rewards will be terrific. That's the argument to use. If it were me, I'd go to men like Charlie Oatman and Joe Evans and dare them to stay out . . . You're smiling. Does it sound so ridiculous?"

"Not at all!" Rocky was very emphatic; she had given him an idea and doubt was gone from his mind.

"Naturally, Frank and I haven't talked anything but oil all day," he continued. "I was so sold on the idea that I let my enthusiasm run away with me. I didn't say anything to Frank, but on the way in I began to back down. You've put me on the right track, Rita. I'll get together with him tomorrow and work out something. By the time you come home from Texas, I'll be ready to shoot."

8

GRIMWOOD CAME TO ROCKY'S OFFICE THE FOLLOWING afternoon with an agreement that proved to be satisfactory to both. They signed it and Rocky turned over a thousand dollars in cash.

"I won't need that much," Grimwood said. "I don't expect to pay over two dollars an acre for the land."

"You'll need something for expenses. If you have to grease somebody's palm, do it. You're not busy in court right now. Why don't you grab a train in the morning and run down to Cheyenne and close the deal as quickly as you can? That'll beat exchanging letters and wasting a month."

"All right," Grimwood agreed. "I shouldn't be gone more than three or four days." Grinning, he added, "When you get interested, you move fast, don't you?"

"I'll try not to trip myself," Rocky observed, and he wasn't thinking only of the business in hand.

Grimwood left the next morning. With both Frank

and Tony away, Rocky found himself at a loose end. He went out to the lake on Tuesday evening but found no one there who interested him, and after a swim, returned to town. He considered going to the Spanish Ranch, only to decide that it was too soon.

On Thursday, as he was on his way to the weekly luncheon of the Business Men's Club, he ran into Tony on Bridger Street. He hadn't expected her back for another day or two.

"This is a surprise," he told her. "I wasn't looking for you until Friday."

"Then, you *were* looking for me?" she asked, banteringly.

"Naturally," he said, and both laughed. It gave Rocky a lift to see her again. "But why back so soon?"

"Oh, things went my way. I found a bandy-legged puncher by the name of Shorty Hicks at the ranch. He was exactly what I wanted and proved to be an excellent model. He has an old bald-faced roan in his string that I couldn't have improved on for the picture. The weather was fine—not too hot and very little wind. We left for the Blue Rock late on Monday and didn't get back to Taylors' until last evening. Shorty was a jewel. He did the cooking and babied me scandalously."

Rocky wasn't interested in hearing her sing Shorty's praises.

"And the picture—it's finished?"

"Just about."

That was shading the truth considerably. Her curiosity (that's what she chose to call it) regarding what was transpiring in Boulder City, as it pertained to Rita

Warren, had become so disturbing that it had driven her home ahead of time.

"What have you been doing, Rocky?"

"Not much of anything since Sunday. Frank's in Cheyenne. We had an interesting day in the desert. On the way back, we stopped at the Spanish Ranch and had dinner with Rita."

"Rita?" Tony echoed, and her chin went up an inch or two. "She's very hospitable—and charming."

Rocky nodded. He had no alternative. Without half trying, Tony had got under his guard and trapped him.

"It was a very enjoyable evening," he responded lamely. And then, with sudden resolve, "I'm looking forward to seeing the ranch. She promised to show me over it the next time.

"You mustn't wait until she's gone. Rita won't be home for long."

Tony's solicitude was sweet and cutting. Rocky pretended not to notice its sharp edge.

"I'm anxious to see what you've done," he said. "I wish I could ask you to lunch, but this is club day."

"This *is* Thursday," she said, as though just recollecting the fact. "I won't keep you, Rocky. I hope you have an interesting speaker. I'll be seeing you around."

She was gone then. He had expected her to ask him up to the house that evening. He was both glad and sorry that she hadn't.

"She's quick on the trigger," he thought, continuing on to the hotel. "All I had to do was open my mouth and she had me figured out."

The club meetings were always well attended. The

chair was a revolving office, which provided a new chairman every week. His chief responsibility was to provide an interesting speaker. Usually, there was someone in Boulder City for a day or two who could be induced to address the club. The high-water mark was reached when the chairman came up with a U.S. Senator or a Congressman. When no visitor was available, some local character reluctantly offered himself as a sacrifice. Rock bottom had been struck when Chet Purdy, the town's leading mortician had filled in. Not only was Chet's trade on the grim side, but he had an impediment in his speech that was annoying even when he quoted the price on a funeral. He spoke at length on the history of embalming. Though the members had suffered through it without listening, no one had ever forgotten it.

Sheriff Ty Roberts was the chairman today. He and the other members were already at the table when Rocky slipped in and took his accustomed seat. Ty had a guest, a middle-aged man of rather serious mien, who, obviously, was to address the club. Rocky had never seen him before.

"Who have we got with us today?" he inquired of Louie Abramson, the proprietor of the Bon Ton Department Store, who sat at his right.

"An old friend of Ty's," Louie replied. "His name is Conlan. He's from Denver."

"Denver, eh?" Rocky was only mildly interested.

"Yeh, Denver Police Department. He's a lieutenant of detectives."

Rocky was all interest now. His glance ran around the long table and came to rest on Charlie Oatman.

The latter did not look his way. He was carrying on a conversation across the table with Doc Wingaard and gave no indication that he had anything of a sinister nature on his mind.

It didn't satisfy Rocky. His gray eyes darkened with suspicion as the feeling grew on him that bringing a lieutenant of detectives from Denver had no other purpose than to unmask him. The rest of it was just a cleverly arranged trick.

His appetite gone, he toyed with his food as he waited, his guard up, but not knowing just what was to come.

Half an hour passed before Ty got to his feet and banged his fist on the table for quiet.

"We're lucky today, gentlemen," he began. "I've got an old friend of mine here to talk to you. He's on his way to the Coast to address a conference of police chiefs. He stopped off between trains to see me, and I promptly hog-tied him and got him up here. You've all heard somethin' about fingerprintin'. In the big cities, all the police departments are usin' it. In Washington, the Department of Justice is goin' all out on it. It's the best thing has ever been discovered for identifying criminals. It's sure-fire. You can finger-print known crooks and send the information all over the country. But that's only half of it; if it's murder or robbery, the guilty party may think he's left no clues behind. If his fingerprints are there, the police find them, and they're the best clue they could have. But I'm goin' to let Mike go into that. He's the fingerprint expert for the Denver police ... Gentlemen, Lieutenant Mike Conlan."

Ty's introductory remarks rubbed none of the suspicion out of Rocky's mind. He had never been arrested, never fingerprinted. Undoubtedly he had left his prints around. They could have been found. But if that was what he had to face, why this elaborate build-up? Roberts could have found him at his office and taken him down to the jail without all this beating around the bush.

In spite of his preoccupation, Rocky found the lieutenant's remarks of great interest. So did the other members of the club. When he concluded, he received a long round of enthusiastic applause. He was still on his feet, and when he got their attention, he said:

"I happened to mention to Ty that I had an ink pad and dusting powder with me. He thought you boys would get a kick out of it if you stepped up, one at a time, and had me fingerprint you. I'll be able to tell you which one of the four categories you belong in. But that's about all; I can't quarantee you that you'll go straight or end up behind the bars."

The majority voiced their approval; it was a lark and they were for it.

"This is it," thought Rocky. "If I refuse to be printed, it'll be a dead giveaway. If I go through with it, they'll compare the prints with some they've got and I'll be tabbed."

He didn't doubt for a moment but what this was Oatman's work.

"I didn't think he'd take a chance. He knows I can pull him down, too . . . I don't get it!"

To his surprise, when it came Oatman's turn to be

fingerprinted, the president of the First National hung back.

"I don't approve of this at all," he declared nervously. "We shouldn't be doing it. Fingerprinting is a serious business. We're making a joke of it."

"What are you afraid of, Charlie?" Joe Evans demanded, with a raucous laugh.

Others began to twit him and Ty joined in.

"You got a skeleton in your closet, Charlie?"

"No, I haven't!" Oatman snapped. He put out his hands and was printed, though he continued to protest.

A scornful smile touched Rocky's face.

"Figured at the last moment that they might have found his prints, too," he told himself. "If he had any sense, he'd have kept his mouth shut; his prints are all over the bank, and he's got a perfect alibi for them."

Rocky didn't hold back when it came his turn to walk up to the ink pad. He caught Oatman watching him intently. The actor in Rocky came to the surface and he grinned back impudently.

It was over and done with then. The members gathered around Conlan to hear what he had to tell them. Rocky waited; but nothing happened. In a few minutes, the meeting broke up and he went back to his office.

There was no lessening of tension in him. Every time he heard footsteps in the hall, he expected to have them stop at his door. Sitting at his desk, smoking cigarette after cigarette, he heard the main line train for the west pull out at 3:05. If Lieutenant Conlan had lived up to his announced intention, he was on it.

Rocky began watching the clock. When another

twenty minutes had passed, he clapped on his hat and went directly to the sheriff's office. He found Roberts there. Ty had just come back from seeing his friend off.

"That was a fine meeting, Rocky. Everybody had a good time." Ty checked himself on noticing Rocky's serious demeanor. "What's on yore mind?"

"Ty, what was the purpose behind that fingerprinting? Was it aimed at me?"

"At you? Of course not! It wasn't aimed at nobody. What gave you that idea?"

Rocky dissembled his relief.

"I don't know," he said. "I'm the only new member of the club. Been here just a few weeks. I thought maybe Oatman was behind it, figuring it would embarrass me."

"No!" Ty snorted. "How could it embarrass you? You ain't a crook. Charlie Oatman was the one who was embarrassed."

"I'm glad to hear it," Rocky told him. "What did Conlan do with the prints?"

"He threw 'em in the waste basket here. You want 'em?"

"No," Rocky remarked coolly. "They don't mean anything to me."

He lingered on, making talk that was calculated to cover up what had gone before. He and Ty had always got on well together. He knew the sheriff's fondness for a good story. It wasn't long before he had Ty holding his sides with laughter.

Dade Hollister, Ty's deputy, came in as they sat there. Dade drew up a chair and had just begun to trade stories with them, when a smallish Negro brought a lathered horse to a slithering stop at the door and ran in excitedly. He was Press Totter, one of Crissy's sons, from the Spanish Ranch.

"Mistah Sheriff, you gotta come quick to the ranch! An' you gotta fetch the doctor!"

"Take it easy, Press," Ty counseled. He was on his feet at once. "What's happened?"

Press had to catch his breath before he could continue.

"Mistah Roberts, you know that Indian, Jim Bucktoe, who works for Miz Warren. He's been actin' funny fer a long time. He got a knife somewheres this afternoon and went after a couple exercise boys. Lonnie and Stub didn't have no trouble with him before. Jim didn't have no reason to use a knife on 'em. I reckon he's just gone plumb crazy. Stub's cut up awful bad."

"Is that all?" Ty snapped.

"No, suh. Mistah Fitz and his wife is away. Jim got into their house and stole a rifle and a bagful of ca'tridges. He fired a lot of shots that didn't hit nobody. We could hear him yellin' that he's kill anyone that got in his way. The last we saw of him, he was headin' in the direction of the Slate Hills. Miz Warren's afraid he'll come back tonight and none of us will be safe."

"We'll go after him," said Ty. "You find Pete Hoffman, Dade. Tell him I want him to go with us. How about you, Rocky?"

"I'll be glad to go, Ty. You can fix me up with a rifle?"

"Sure! You locate Doc Wingaard and have him here inside of ten minutes. We'll have the horses saddled and be ready to ride by the time you get back. Try Doc's house first; he's usually home nappin', this time of the afternoon."

Rocky left on the double-quick.

"This is good, me riding with the law," he muttered.

He thought of Rita, menaced by a madman, and it squeezed all the humor out of him.

"Be a hell of a note having some dumb Injun go crazy and ruin everything I've got lined up!" He broke into a run, growling, "Too damn bad Roberts hasn't got a railroad engine handy so he could go after this bird the way he chased me!"

9

RITA SAW THEM COMING AND RAN OUT WHEN THEY
dashed into the yard. Rocky hit the ground before the
others and rushed up to her.

"Are you all right?" he demanded anxiously.

"Yes, I'm all right, or will be as soon as I can pull
myself together," she replied, with a sigh of relief.
"It's been a terrible experience."

Rocky squeezed her hand and said, "Take it easy,
Rita."

Though badly shaken, she managed a smile for him.
Ty reached her then. She thanked him for coming so
promptly and had a nod for Wingaard and the others.

"Has he been back, Mrs. Warren?" the sheriff
asked.

"No, thank heaven! I felt so helpless with Mr.
Fitz away. All of Ted's guns are in the case. I loaded
one. I was afraid to pass out the others. I thought if
that maniac did come back, the sight of guns would
send him on another rampage. It isn't as though I had

a bunch of cowboys here who could handle a situation like this."

Ty asked Press to point out the direction the Indian had taken.

"Last I saw of him, Mistah Roberts, he was dog-trottin' through the brush on that slope ovah there."

"He wasn't workin' west a bit, as though he was goin' to cross the tracks?"

"No, suh."

"Wal, I dunno," Ty muttered, thinking aloud. "He's most likely figgerin' to skirt around the hills and git across the Dry Crick range and down to the Reservation. An Injun will hate the Reservation, but nine times out of ten, when he gits in trouble, he'll head for it. We'll fan out of here and see if we can't pick him up. Doc will stay till we git back, Mrs. Warren . . . What shape are those two boys in?"

"I'm sure Lonnie will make it. I don't know about Stub."

"Let me have a look at them—and the sooner the better," said Wingaard.

Roberts nodded.

"Can we git through that upper fence?" he inquired.

"Yes, there's a gate," Rita told him.

"Okay!" Ty grumbled. "Let's go!"

Rocky had a word with Rita before he swung up.

"You'll be perfectly safe with Wingaard here," he declared reassuringly. "Doc knows how to use a gun."

"Of course," she murmured, her eyes lingering on his. "Thanks for being so thoughtful, Rocky."

He looked back as he rode away and saw her hurrying down the yard with Wingaard and Press. He was the last man through the gate. The others had held up to get Ty's instructions.

"We'll swing through the lower hills," Roberts told them. "If Joe's kept on the move, he's a long ways ahead of us by now. George Twigg has a little hay ranch on Stony Crick. We'll stop there and find out if they've seen anythin' of him. And another thing," he added, as they were about to pull away. "We're dealin' with a madman. Don't take no chances with him; he won't throw down his gun if we git him surrounded."

"We'll be lucky if we see him first," Pete Hoffman remarked. "He'll lay out in the brush or behind a clump of rocks and pick us off if he can."

"Yeh," Ty agreed, "that's what we got to look out for."

They spread out as they moved away from the fence, riding slowly and scrutinizing every outcropping and likely looking spot for an ambush before they approached it.

Off to his right, Rocky could see the Blue Rock stretching away to the horizon. A blanket of hot air lay over it, shimmering in the glare of the sun and rising and falling sluggishly, like an oily sea on a calm afternoon.

He jerked his attention away from it quickly and riveted it on the slope ahead. With his rifle resting lightly in the crook of his left arm, he touched his horse with his heels and drew abreast of the others.

They covered three miles or more in that fashion, uphill and down, without seeing anything of Indian Joe. Another low crest intervened. They topped it, and at the bottom came to a narrow, dusty hill road. Ty held up his hand and they stopped.

"We better have a little parley," he declared. "We've come quite a piece. That Injun may still be ahead of us, or he might have been cute enough to turn back to the railroad, after all, and be hoofing it up the tracks . . . What do you think, Dade?"

"I thought your first guess was the right one, Ty. I believe Joe's heading for the Reservation. He wouldn't wander out into the desert."

Pete Hoffman nodded his agreement with this. Rocky had no opinion to offer.

"But this road," he said. "Where does it go?"

"In the direction yo're lookin', it runs into the Spanish Ranch road," Roberts informed him.

"I didn't see it cutting in, when Frank and I went out to the Blue Rock last Sunday."

"Wal, it does—'bout a mile east of the house. It's faint in places. Hardpan. It's what we call Twigg's road. He's the only one uses it." Ty was studying the road as he spoke. "A team and wagon passed along here since sunup. Twigg, or young George, must have lit out early for town."

He got down heavily.

"You boys wait up here a bit and I'll walk ahead a few yards. If Joe's usin' the road, he's left some sign."

He was gone only a few minutes.

"Couldn't find a thing," he announced, on his return. "We'll stick to the road as far as Twigg's place. Keep yore eyes peeled; that Injun may have cut across somewheres ahead."

They went on, but for less than a half-a-mile, when

Dade Hollister reined up sharply and pointed at the dust.

"What do you make of that?" he asked Ty.

"They're fresh prints, boys!" Roberts was elated. "We guessed right this time!"

Swinging around a bend, a comparatively long stretch of road opened before them. Over it came a wildly driven horse. A woman was in the saddle, riding astride, her skirts flapping about her knees. In her arms she clutched a child of eight or nine.

Though it could hardly have been anyone else, Roberts waited until he recognized her.

"Good Lord!" he groaned. "That's Elvira Twigg! She wouldn't be ridin' that way if there wasn't somethin' wrong!"

The others exchanged glances and were of one mind as to what had happened. Rocky put it into words.

"Injun Joe!" he said, his voice hard and flat.

It wasn't necessary to say any more.

In a matter of seconds, Ty was questioning the frantic woman. He found her so distraught she could barely speak.

"Joe Bucktoe, Vira?" he inquired, trying to help her out.

"Yes," she sobbed. "He killed George, Mr. Roberts, right before my eyes! How could he have done it? How could he? We never did anything but befriend Joe. Even after he quit working for us, he was always welcome. The only reason we let him go was because we just couldn't afford to keep him on any longer. We thought he understood, and now he's come and killed George."

Her grief overcame her and she couldn't go on. The little girl in her arms was crying wildly. Ty tried to comfort the child, but she drew away from him and clutched her mother all the tighter.

"Vira—when did this happen?" If Ty sounded stern it was because he knew no better way to proceed.

"'Bout forty minutes ago," Mrs. Twigg got out chokingly. "No more'n that, Mr. Roberts . . . You mustn't carry on like that, Phoebe," she told the little girl. "This is Mr. Roberts, the sheriff. He'll take Joe away."

"Now, if you'll tell me just what happened, Vira, I'll be able to proceed," Ty declared brusquely. "I don't want to bear down on you, but you've got to pull yoreself together for a minute."

It had the desired effect.

"Why, that Joe crept up behind the woodpile," Mrs. Twigg explained. "I was in the kitchen, peeling potatoes. Through the window, I could see George coming up from the barn. There was a shot, and he went down. Joe straightened up, holding a rifle. Not a word had passed between them. No quarrel, no nothing; it was just murder."

The wretched woman had to pause and steel herself before she could continue.

"Joe saw me at the window and started to run to the house. We've always kept a loaded shotgun in the kitchen. I got it and emptied both barrels at him. I stung him, but I couldn't have hurt him much, 'cause he turned and hustled back to the woodpile. He began shooting at me. A couple bullets came through the window. I made the baby lay on the floor. Ever so

92

often I'd shove the shotgun over sill and pull the trigger. I knew I couldn't hold him off with a shotgun for long, but I had to do something."

The courage of this thin, sharp-featured woman, with her scraggly blond hair and the marks of hard work stamped on her roughened hands and bony shoulders, won Rocky's admiration. He knew something about the hopelessness and grinding poverty that fell to the lot of a woman on a small, back country hay ranch. Money was so hard to come by, that to make a precious dollar, it was no wonder they often fed a hard-pressed stranger and then forgot to tell the sheriff.

How Mrs. Twigg had managed to reach a horse and escape unharmed puzzled Rocky. Ty got around to asking her, presently.

"George's horse was standing at the hitch rack at the side of the house," she replied. "It was out of the line of fire from the woodpile. I thought if I could get through an open window on that side, with the baby, I could mount and make a run for it. That's what I did. I stuck the shotgun out again and fired. Joe began banging away once more. Quick as I could, I crawled through a window and got in the saddle. I pulled Phoebe up with me and lit out fast."

Ty complimented her on using her head. And then:

"Young George is in town, I take it."

"He left home about four o'clock this morning. And that's another thing; I was afraid he'd drive up this evening, not knowing anything was wrong, and Joe would kill him, too."

"You don't have to worry about that now, Vira,"

said Ty. "We'll stop him at the Spanish Ranch. I want you to go on to the ranch. Mrs. Warren will take you in. Stay there till we show up. Understand?"

"Yes—"

"Then git movin', Vira. We'll take care of Joe Bucktoe," he promised.

Rocky swung up alongside of Ty as Mrs. Twigg drew away.

"You figure that Injun is still at her place?"

"Most likely. He was hired man there; he's boss now. That'll hold him a while. When he gits through pickin' up what he wants, he may burn the house. We'll know directly. It ain't over a couple miles to Twigg's. What wind there is is blowin' in the other direction, or we'd have heard the shootin'."

He held them back a moment while he considered what course to pursue with Bucktoe.

"That'll be best," he muttered, confirming the decision he had reached. "Stony Crick flows across the road. There ain't more'n a trickle of water in it this time of the year. But the crick bed is there. We'll go up it. That'll put us a hundred yards or so behind the barn. When we git that far, we'll figger out our next move."

They reached the creek without incident and found it so low that what water there was had settled in the deeper pools, leaving stretches of dry sand in between. Through the fringe of willows that screened the stream, they could see the forlorn-looking little house and the small barn, the latter even more down-at-the-heel than the house, a side board or two missing and the warped, sun-baked shingles seemingly ready to be scattered by the first severe storm that struck them.

Ty led the way, moving cautiously and repeatedly warning the others to do the same. Rocky saw him raise a hand and point to the rear of the house. The woodpile could be seen now. Something lay on the ground between it and the barn. Knowing what to look for, there was no mistaking it for what it was, even at that distance.

Rocky heard Dade Hollister say, "That's him." And Pete Hoffman said, "His old woman won't have to sew no more patches on his pants."

10

They continued up the creek until they were behind the barn.

"He ain't spotted us yet," said Ty. "We'd have drawn a shot before this if he had."

"If he's still here, you mean," Pete observed.

"He's awful quiet if he's in there," said Dade. "I don't know whether George kept a bottle in the house or not. If he did, it's a cinch Joe found it. He may be stretched out on the floor, dead drunk.

Roberts shook his head. "No bottle ever held whisky enough to lay him out."

Rocky was silent. The sheriff glanced at him inquiringly.

"You're doing the dealing, Ty."

Roberts nodded appreciatively. "We'll settle this in a hurry."

Raising his rifle, he fired a shot in the air. It brought a vicious response. From inside the house, a rifle cracked on one side and then on the other. A third shot came from the rear kitchen window. A growl of satisfaction escaped Ty.

"He's hoppin' around in there like a jack rabbit! All we got to do now is dig him out of his hole."

"No trick to that," Pete Hoffman declared rashly. "We can leave the broncs here and walk right up to the barn. If we get down on our bellies, we can crawl the rest of the way to the woodpile."

Ty shook his head. Rocky didn't wait for him to voice an objection; he had something of his own to say now.

"That doesn't make sense to me, Pete. Suppose we get as close in as the woodpile. We'll be hung up there, without so much as a blade of grass between us and the house. That Injun knocked Twigg off with his first shot, so he ain't so crazy he can't use a gun."

"He'd drop one or two of us off for sure if we tried to rush him from the woodpile," said Roberts. "We'll have to come up with something better than that. There's four of us. If we got in position so we could work up on three sides of the house, while the fourth man forted up in the barn and covered the rear, we'd gradually wear him down; he couldn't be in four places at once."

"That's as safe a way as any," Rocky conceded, "but it'll be slow work." He shaded his eyes and glanced at the sun. "We haven't too much daylight left. If we didn't wind it up before nightfall, our gun flashes would give him something to shoot at."

"You got somethin' better to suggest?" Ty demanded, a little crusty now.

"Not better but quicker," said Rocky. "If the three

97

of you get into the barn and throw lead into the kitchen, I'll go back down the creek and get around in front of the place. It must be three hundred yards from the creek bottom to the front door. That'll give me room enough to throw the prod into my horse and really get moving. When I flash past the house, I'll leap off and try to hit the door. There's no porch or steps to get in my way. If you keep the Injun busy, it'll give me a few seconds to pull myself together before I bust in on him."

"No, no, I won't let you take that chance!" Ty objected. "But I admire yore guts in offerin' to play it that way, Rocky."

Dade and Pete nodded, and Dade said, "Reckon you've got the nerve to get away with it, at that."

Rocky smiled grimly.

"If I didn't think I could get away with it, I wouldn't mention it."

"Maybe Joe will be obliging enough to make a run for it and save us the trouble of going in to get him," Dade remarked. He wasn't speaking facetiously but his tone indicated how little hope he entertained that Bucktoe would try to break away.

Another shot came from the house, from the front this time, and then several more from a window that overlooked the creek.

"Still tryin' to locate us," Ty growled. "I'm goin' up to the barn; you wait here."

The three men watched him as he moved away with a determined stride and saw him reach the barn and try to squeeze through an opening a missing board had left.

98

Ty couldn't make it and had to pry off another board before he got through. Once inside, he walked across the dirt floor and studied the house briefly through a crack. At greater length, he carefully scanned the flat, hoping to find a shallow ditch or other break in the flinty surface that would offer a man at least some cover.

He found nothing that would serve the purpose.

"Ain't even a gopher hole out there!" he muttered.

His eyes narrowed grimly as they came back to the stiff, grotesque shape of George Twigg.

"Too bad!" thought Ty. "Thank God, Elvira's got young George to look out for her and the little girl."

He glanced around him at the contents of the barn. There were the usual odds and ends of harness and tools, the parts of a mowing machine that Twigg had been repairing, and the wheels and running gear of a wagon, on which a rack could be placed, when hay was being harvested. Ty tried to find a box for the wagon, and failed. Once, in Quinn Valley, he and a posse had loaded a wagon with bagged sand and pushed it up against a cabin, in which a killer was making his stand, and had taken the man out without firing a shot.

Ty took a minute to think things over. He didn't often reverse himself, but this situation left him no choice. By the time he reached the creek, his mind was made up. Without preamble, he said, "Rocky, you still ready to go after that Injun?"

"Sure," Rocky answered, without hesitation.

"Wal, you know the chances yo're takin'. I ain't askin' you to put yoreself on the spot, you understand. If I wasn't stumped, I wouldn't even consider lettin' you go. That flat's as smooth as a billard table; not a crack in it." The sheriff shook his head soberly. "There's one dead man out there already; I don't have to tell you to be careful."

Rocky nodded and said, "I'll be all right. Give me about fifteen minutes to get down the creek. In the meantime, the three of you get inside the barn and throw a shot or two at the back window. When I hear you open up full blast, I'll make my break. A rifle won't be any use to me. Let me have your .44."

"Just a minute," Pete Hoffman protested. "No reason why you should take this on yourself. Suppose we draw straws. Whoever gets the short one will be the man to go."

Ty promptly vetoed the suggestion.

"I thought of that. It's got to be Rocky or no one; I'm too old to git away with it, and so are you and Dade. I didn't use to think anything of leapin' off a runnin' hoss. If I saw I wasn't goin' to land on my feet, I'd throw myself into a roll and come up with nothin' worse than a skinned shoulder . . . You don't do those things after you've passed fifty."

That ended it. He handed Rocky his gun. The latter broke it open and tried the trigger action. After taking up another notch on the cinch straps, he mounted and began picking his way down the creek bed.

He was on his own now. When rifles cracked in the barn, he didn't tighten up.

"This won't be too tough," he told himself. "If I hit that door just right, I'll be inside and have it over with in a hurry."

When he had gone far enough to gain an angle on

which to race across the flat without exposing himself unnecessarily to gunfire from the side of the house, he began looking for a break in the fringe of willows. He found such a spot. Screened there, he waited several minutes. The cracking of rifles in the barn began to swell to a steady tattoo. Answering shots came from the kitchen.

This was the moment. Heeling his horse, Rocky broke into the open and lifted his mount into a driving gallop. Flattened out on the animal's neck, he reached the front of the house without drawing a shot. His timing was perfect, and when he leaped, he landed on his feet, only to crash against the door with impact enough to snap the latch. He tried to save himself, but he was only pawing the air, and when he hit the floor, he was halfway across the front room.

In the moment that he lay there, he knew he was hurt. There was agony in his left shoulder and a knifing pain in his ribs.

The connecting door to the rear stood ajar. It was flung open with a bang. Joe Bucktoe stood there. Gobbling like a turkey, he half-raised his rifle and fired. . .

Rocky was on his knees. The slug screamed past his head and ploughed into the wall. He squeezed the trigger of the .44 again and again. The rifle slipped from the Indian's fingers and he tried to keep himself erect by clutching the door frame. Life had gone out of him, however, and he crumpled to the floor.

Rocky was still on his knees when Ty burst in. The sheriff's quick glance ran from the riddled body of the Indian to Rocky.

"You fetched him!" he exclaimed. "I knew you would. And you—you all right?"

"I'm still all in one piece, but I suspect I cracked a rib. My left shoulder is all fouled up, too. I hit the door so hard the bolt snapped and I busted in here like I was shot out of a cannon . . . Help me to get up, Ty. Don't touch that left side!"

Dade and Pete came in in time to hear his story of what had happened. He was in great pain and couldn't conceal the fact.

"It wouldn't do any good for me to have a look at your shoulder," said Ty. "The thing to do is to git you back to the Spanish Ranch and let Doc Wingaard go over you . . . Do you think you can ride?"

"I can ride if you boys will set me in the saddle."

"We'll do that." Ty turned to Dade. "You and Pete catch up his bronc, and I'll git started back with him. I want the two of you to stick around until I can git the coroner and Chet Purdy out here. That ought to be about midnight. Locate a blanket and cover George up." He jerked his head to indicate Joe Bucktoe. "You can leave this fellow right where he is. Thanks to Rocky, we're all breathin' regular. We can count ourselves lucky, I reckon."

It was a slow and painful ride to the Spanish Ranch for Rocky. Wingaard put him to bed and diagnosed his injuries as a broken rib and dislocated shoulder. He called Ty in to assist him and set the shoulder at once.

"That must feel better," he said.

"Sure does," Rocky agreed, "but it's still sore as hell. How long am I going to be laid up, Doc?"

"Why, you'll be as good as new in a few days. I'll tape up that rib when I get you into town. In the meantime, don't try to bend over or put any strain on it." Doc chuckled. "You're going to be buttonholed by everybody you run into, Rocky. Having to tell your story over and over, thirty to forty times a day, will pester you more than your fractured rib."

Rita appeared in the doorway and asked if she could come in.

"Certainly," Ty told her. "The boy's full of aches, but he's goin' to be as good as ever in a few days. Doc was just sayin' that he's goin' to have more trouble with folks makin' a hero of him than with his busted rib. But mebbe that won't be so hard to take." Ty winked at Rocky. "The young cuss deserves a spot in the limelight."

"I should think so," said Rita. "We'll keep him here tonight, of course."

Wingaard advised against it. He explained why.

"I fought for years for a county hospital. Now that we have one, I want my patients to have the benefit of its advantages—not that I'll keep this boy there long. If you'll supply a rig, I'll get him into town."

"Gladly," Rita assured him. "I'll have Press hitch the surrey." She smiled at Rocky. "We'll send you in in state."

After doing what he could for Stub and Lonnie, the two Negro lads who had been attacked by the Indian, Wingaard had them taken to Boulder City, also.

"I know you're anxious about Stub, Mrs. Warren," he said. "I'll send word back by Press. But don't expect too much; he's got a fighting chance, that's all."

Old Posie came to the door and spoke to the sheriff. Young George Twigg had just been stopped as he was passing the house.

"I'll talk to him," said Ty. He turned to Rita. "Mrs. Warren, is it goin' to inconvenience you to take the three of 'em in for the night?"

"Not at all," she told him. "I'm more than willing to do all I can. I don't suppose they have any money for the funeral."

"They ain't likely to have. Of course, there's always the County—"

Rita shook her head. "I don't want that. You tell young George I'll help them out. In a way, I feel responsible."

"No reason why you should," said Ty. "But it's decent of you—awful decent, Mrs. Warren, to offer to help them."

When he stepped out, Wingaard left with him.

Rita walked over to Rocky and sat down on the bed.

"You were as good as your word," she said tenderly, her hand cool on his forehead.

He gazed at her for a long moment, his pains and aches temporarily forgotten.

"I don't get you," he murmured.

"The other evening—what you said to Frank and me. You remember, about giving a good account of yourself if the chips were down and there was gunsmoke at the end of it? I believe I'm quoting you."

Rocky grinned. "I say a lot of things, Rita. You can believe me, when I say I admire the way you handled yourself today. No going to pieces for you."

"You don't know how close I was to it," she said.

"I looked up the road a thousand times this afternoon, when I thought it was time for you to be returning, and you didn't come . . . I didn't want anything to happen to you."

She bent down suddenly and brushed his cheek with her lips. His good right arm caught her and held her close.

"Please—" she whispered. "I shouldn't have done that. I—I'm still bewildered, I guess."

"So am I," he said, with sudden fire. "I can't believe this has happened to me."

He turned her face and his lips found her mouth.

11

NEXT MORNING, PROPPED UP IN HIS HOSPITAL BED and resting comfortably, Rocky was promptly made aware of the new esteem in which he was held. Don Pierce, the editor of the *Mercury*, was his first visitor. In the course of his interview, he said that everyone in Boulder City was singing Rocky's praises.

This was a slight overstatement, for across town at the moment, as he sat at breakfast with Tony and his wife, Charlie Oatman was registering a demurrer.

"You can't deny that he's got nerve, Father," Tony insisted.

"Oh, sure, he's got nerve," Oatman conceded. "No question about that. Roberts was there on the spot; he could have handled the situation. Jeanette saw his chance to make a grandstand play, and he took advantage of it. I suppose you women will be falling all over him now."

Celia Oatman laughed.

"Charles, you give up hard. Rocky can have anything he wants in a business way, in this town now. If you're half as shrewd as I've always believed you to be, you won't try to hold out against him."

Scowling to himself, Oatman went down to the bank. Why hadn't Indian Joe Bucktoe taken more careful aim? According to the story being told of what had happened at the Twiggs' place, he had had Rocky at his mercy for a moment. A shot in the right place would have done the trick.

"It would have made everything all right for me," was Charlie's brooding thought. "Now, he's on top of the heap and I'll never be rid of him."

Tony went to the hospital, just before eleven. She had convinced herself that it was foolish to be piqued with Rocky. After all, they had never been anything more than good friends.

"I won't be juvenile about it," she thought. "It isn't as though I were in love with him."

Rocky was happy to see her. He couldn't understand why he always got a lift out of seeing her and found himself regretting certain things he had done and which were now long past any undoing.

Tony had been there only a few minutes, when Mrs. Warren arrived. Rocky caught the icy sweetness with which they greeted each other. Rita's attitude toward him was possessive, and intentionally so. He listened as they talked and could feel Tony drawing back into her shell.

Beneath his smiling mask Rocky regarded them with the same keen interest with which a gambler studies his cards. Tony had a drag for him that he couldn't deny. But Rita, wealthy, beautiful and willing, had everything a man could want in a woman. There wasn't any doubt in his mind as to the course he would take. Rita was his golden opportunity; she would solve all his problems. He was eager to embrace it, and reluctant, too. It puzzled him. He gave up trying to understand it; for once, he'd play it smart.

"I'll make sure of it now," he thought. "This is where the road forks. It'll be better if Tony understands it."

He didn't want to hurt her. With what he thought was great subtlety, he began turning the conversation over to Rita, first about Stub's condition and then on to her horses and Hannibal's chances at Denver. Rita obliged him with a neat assist.

"I brought Crissy in with me," she said. "We met Dr. Wingaard at the door. He says Stub is doing better than holding his own."

"I'm glad to hear it," he returned. "I don't suppose anything like yesterday will come up again, but you ought to have a man on the ranch that you can depend on."

Rita smiled and said, her meaning not too obscure, "Maybe I will have—some day."

On the matter of her horses she had a great deal to say.

"When you see the Warren colors go to the post, you can be sure the stable is betting, Rocky. I know what Hannibal will have to face at Denver. I expect him to have a rather easy time of it . . . Why don't you come down? You can spare a few days."

"I'm going to be busy—"

"So you are," she cut in. "I forgot."

Tony knew she was being left out, and not by accident. Rocky's clumsy subterfuge had not fooled her for a moment. She was infuriated but dissembled it perfectly.

"I'm afraid I can't talk thoroughbreds with you—having had so little experience with them," she spoke up. There was a barb in her words for Rocky, and he got it.

"You're not going already?" Rita inquired, as Tony arose.

"I hate to tear myself away, but I have some work laid out for today." Tony gave Rocky an enigmatic smile. "I'm sure you won't be neglected."

"I'll see you again, Tony?"

"Naturally—if I can crowd in," she said lightly.

She was gone, then, and he only half heard the compliment Rita paid her.

"I don't know what I'm worrying about," he thought. "This is the way I wanted it—exactly what I asked for."

The nurse came to the door to tell him Louie Abramson and three other gentlemen were waiting to see him.

"What about the barber, Miss Karns?"

"He's here, too."

"Well, tell them to wait a minute," Rocky told her. "Mike can shave me while the rest of us are gabbing."

Rita had him alone for a few moments more.

"You haven't heard anything from Frank?" she asked.

"Not yet."

"I hope things go his way. I imagine they will. Frank's as unpretentious and comfortable as an old shoe, but he gets things done ... He and Tony make a fine couple. I suppose you've noticed."

She bent down to kiss him good-by. Rocky held on to her.

"You don't have to be jealous of Tony Oatman," he murmured.

"No?" she queried, with a little laugh. "I hope Frank Grimwood will never have any reason to be jealous of you."

The routine of the day set a pattern for those that followed. Rita came every day. On Sunday, Tony visited him. To make sure he wouldn't construe it as anything personal, she came with Jinny Evans and another girl.

Sunday evening brought Grimwood back to Boulder City. The *Mercury* had done its best by Rocky and the late and unlamented Joe Bucktoe. Frank had read every line while in Cheyenne. As a result, he went directly from the train to the hospital.

"I knew I'd find you here," he declared as he shook Rocky's hand. "According to what I've been reading, you had a close call."

"Not too close, Frank. Doc's going to let me get out of here on Tuesday. How did things go in Cheyenne?"

"Fine! I had to take a quarter-section—a hundred and sixty acres—but I got it for two-and-a-half an acre."

"That's swell," Rocky told him. "I was getting worried; it was taking you so long ... What's the next step?"

"The land will have to be surveyed. That's going to

let the cat out of the bag, I'm afraid. Everybody will put two and two together."

"Well, let 'em," said Rocky. "You've got the deal sewed up. Nothing could go wrong with the deed, eh?"

"Not now. The money's been passed. The State Land Office will have a surveyor up here this coming week. I can have the incorporation papers ready for filing before then. I'll have to make another quick trip to Cheyenne," Rocky declared. "Instead of waiting for the story to leak out, we'll touch it off ourselves, and with a bang. What's happened while you were away, Frank, hasn't hurt us a bit; it'll sell some stocks for us."

Grimwood frowned.

"I don't like to look at it that way, but I imagine it's true . . . Have you seen Tony?"

"Yeh, she's dropped in a couple of times. She told me this afternoon that she'd just put the finishing touches on that painting she went out to the Taylors' to do. You know, the one she's going to call The Cross Pull? I'm anxious to see it."

"So am I," said Frank. "I haven't had anything to eat. I didn't even stop to clean up before I came over. I'll get some supper. I want to see Tony for a few minutes. If it's all right with you, I'll come back then and we can talk business as late as you please . . . Those two colored boys still in the hospital?"

"Stub's still here, but Doc says he's out of danger. Rita took the other boy back to the ranch yesterday. It'll be all right for us to sit here and talk tonight."

Tony was on the porch with her mother when Frank came up the walk.

"You're back, finally," she said. "How are things in Cheyenne?"

She was hoping to keep the conversation from centering around Rocky, but before Grimwood had time to speak at any length of his trip, Mrs. Oatman broke in.

"We've had some excitement at home, while you were away, Frank. Rocky—"

"I know," he informed her. "I read all about it in Cheyenne. When I got off the train, I went over to the hospital at once and had a chat with him. I gather that he's getting a little weary of talking about it."

"I imagine he is," said Tony. "I know I'm getting fed up with just listening to the story. We haven't had anything else to talk about since last Thursday."

Grimwood had no reason to suspect the turmoil that had beset her in his absence. Even her mother was unaware of it. Tony was in the habit of throwing herself into her work suddenly. It had not occurred to Mrs. Oatman that it had any significance this time. Genius, she believed, was something that it was just as well not to try to understand.

Hard work had nothing to do with the fact that Tony had arrived at a state of mind which permitted her to believe that Rocky meant nothing to her. He had dash and glamour, and, like some schoolgirl, she had let it run away with her. She was glad she had got hold of herself in time.

Having Frank back fortified her. She was in a mood to enlarge and appreciate his many good qualities and homely virtues. He had the brains and integrity to go far. Already there was talk of sending him to the State Assembly. Washington would be the next step. Best of all, there was fire in him, when aroused, and not of the kind that would leap into flame one minute and burn itself out the next.

"I understand you've been busy," said Grimwood. "Rocky told me you have The Cross Pull finished. When are you going to show it to me?"

"Not for a day or two," she answered. "I thought when Rocky is up and about again, I'd invite Rita and the two of you to dinner and make it a little occasion."

This was to be her way of showing Rocky that he had not hurt her; and, more pointedly, that his pursuit of Rita Warren did not concern her in the slightest. She wanted Rita to understand as much, too.

"That'll be fine," Grimwood told her. "I hope the four of us can get together often."

He asked about her father.

"Joe Evans dropped in for Charles and the two of them walked over to Hank Taylor's place," Mrs. Oatman informed him. "Some business deal, I suppose."

Grimwood didn't stay long. He mentioned that he had promised to return to the hospital and spend an hour with Rocky.

Tony walked to the gate with him, her hand in his.

"I missed you," he said, enormously sober. "Of course, that isn't news. But I'll have some news for you in a day or two. Big news. I know it will please you."

She looked up and searched his eyes in the moonlight, trying to find a clue.

"Am I permitted to guess, Frank?"

"No, I don't want you to guess, Tony; I want it to

come as a surprise. If it goes my way, it'll mean a great deal to the two of us."

Back at the hospital, he found Rocky busy with paper and pencil. Several sheets from the pad had been torn off and were spread over the bed.

"What are you up to now?" Frank asked. "Not computing profits already, I hope."

"I'm trying to find a name for the company. How does this one sound? The Blue Rock Oil and Development Company . . . Here, take a look at it."

He handed Grimwood the sheet of paper on which he had printed the words. The latter tried the name aloud.

"Sounds all right," he said, "but the 'development' part of it takes in a lot of territory. It sort of has a get-rich-quick ring. It might scare somebody off. Just the Blue Rock Oil Company would be more solid."

"Maybe you're right," Rocky agreed, after thinking it over. "We don't want to bite off more than we can chew."

He was unfamiliar with the legal details of incorporating the company. He knew officers had to be named. When that matter came up he insisted that Grimwood put himself down for president.

"This was your baby from the start, Frank, and you can front for it better than I can. Being vice-president will satisfy me. What are we going do about a secretary and treasurer?"

"I did some thinking about it, while I was away," Grimwood replied. "The combination office has to be held by a stockholder. If necessary, I could arrange to have my stenographer put up money enough to buy a share or two. That would comply with the law; but what we really need, Rocky, is a third man to come in with us. I mean someone whose name and cooperation would help us to put the proposition over. If he didn't come in for more than five hundred or a thousand dollars, it would be enough. To get him interested, we could afford to give him some stock as a bonus."

"I don't know," Rocky demurred. "We don't want to split this up so we'll lose control of the company."

"We'll vote ourselves enough stock to make sure that doesn't happen. Don't forget that we've got to raise fifty thousand."

"You've got somebody in mind?"

"Louie Abramson . . . Don't laugh, Rocky. Louie's shrewd and knows how to squeeze a dollar, but he's a born gambler. I know; I've been taking care of his legal work for over a year. I believe if we get him over here tomorrow morning, we can do business with him. The addition he's going to build for the store won't tie him up; Louie's got plenty of money."

Rocky began to like the idea.

"Louie's a smart cookie," he observed. "Nobody's ever seen him throwing his money away. His name on our letterheads ought to convince people that the Blue Rock Oil Company is a good investment . . . You get Louie over here in the morning. We'll be spending hundreds of dollars for grub, when we get going. We can throw that business to his grocery department."

"That'll sound good to Louie," said Frank.

They talked for over an hour. The only reference Rocky made to his real estate and insurance business was to suggest that his office wouldn't do as the headquarters of the oil company.

"There's plenty of space, but we need something on the ground floor. We'd better rent that vacant storeroom across from the Bon Ton. We'll have some signs made to put in the window, with a display of specimens of rock and fossils from Mustard Valley. You'll know what to put in. We'll make this the biggest thing that ever hit Boulder City." He nodded approvingly at the picture he had conjured up in his mind. "It won't be long before the money will be rolling in."

Grimwood smiled at his partner's enthusiasm, but when he spoke it was to utter a word of caution.

"We want to be careful not to get ahead of ourselves. Commitments are all we can take for the present; no money, Rocky, until the incorporation papers have been granted."

It was the first warning he had ever given Rocky. The latter shrugged it off and said, "Sure!"

Next morning, Rita had come and gone before Grimwood arrived at the hospital with Louie. It was almost noon. Louie was apologetic.

"I couldn't get away any sooner, Rocky. You know how it is on Monday, at the store . . . I don't know why I'm here. What you fellas got up your sleeves?"

That opened the doors, and Rocky and Grimwood proceeded to lay their proposition before him. Selling him the idea was not too difficult. Louie's father had come to Boulder City with a pack on his back and had tramped the roads from ranch to ranch for several years, selling notions and jewelry, before his little business warranted the purchase of a horse and wagon. A little store in town had followed. Long before Louie was out of short pants, his father had him behind the counter. Louie had come a long way since those days, and so had the little frame store.

"I'll kick in for a thousand bucks," he told Rocky and Grimwood. "How can I lose? We'll have a crew of freighters and oil well men out there, eating their heads off and wearing out gloves and overalls, all bought at the Bon Ton. Grain will be needed for the horses, and rough timber and dressed lumber for the shacks and the derrick." Louis laughed heartily. "That means more business for me. I'll be even up if all we get out of the well is a little wind."

Though he laughed oftener than most men, he knew how to be serious. He proved it as the conference continued.

"Mrs. Warren is right," he said, commenting on what Rita had told Rocky about selling the venture as a gamble. "Don't try to tell anybody that it's a sure thing. If a man can't afford to lose, tell him to stay out. There'll be plenty who'll take a chance. If the well comes in, a few hundred invested will make a man rich. I don't know why there shouldn't be oil in Wyoming. There's everything else."

"I know we won't bring in a dry well," Grimwood said confidently. "Of course, you never know about oil until you've got it. That'll have to be our story."

"How are you going to break the news?" Louie inquired. "You going to call Don Pierce in and let him play it up in the paper?"

"We may have to handle it that way," said Rocky. "That's if this surveyor shows up before Thursday.

Otherwise, I'm for springing it at the club luncheon. Everybody will be there, and it'll get a great send-off. Don will have time to make his Thursday evening edition with the story."

"That sounds swell to me," Louie declared, with hearty approval. "Charlie Oatman is this week's chairman. He cuts a lot of ice in this town, and especially with Joe Evans and Hank Taylor and that crowd. Get Oatman interested and the rest will be easy."

Grimwood registered an emphatic no.

"You're barking up the wrong tree," he said flatly. "You can forget about Charlie Oatman right now. He'll turn thumbs down on this proposition the moment he hears about it."

"Oh, I don't know about that," Rocky countered.

"Well, I know," Frank insisted. "Just to tell him there may be oil on the Blue Rock makes him see red. He's had me in a couple times and begged me to forget about what he calls 'my oil nonsense.' The last time he had me in, he hinted that he might have to take the bank's business away from me if I didn't give up my rainbow chasing. That's very likely to happen now."

He saw Rocky scowling.

"I told you a long time ago that Charlie Oatman would walk away from this thing, didn't I?"

"You did," Rocky admitted. "I still believe he can be persuaded to change his mind. I'm certainly going to have a talk with him. As far as your losing the bank's legal work, Frank, don't worry about it. I'll guarantee you won't lose it. I'll be out of here tomorrow. In the meantime, you get busy with the papers. And you keep everything under your hat for the present, Louie. If anything comes up and we want to get together in a hurry, we can meet in my office or in Frank's."

Something came up on Tuesday, only it didn't originate with them. Oscar Biberman, the Assemblyman for the Boulder City district, was in Cheyenne, and with an eye on his reelection, made it a practice to send out letters to his prominent constituents. Having found out that Grimwood was purchasing a quarter-section of State land in Mustard Valley, he had sat down and conveyed the information to Charlie Oatman, writing that he was glad to hear there was to be some activity out there. Charlie knew exactly what it meant, and he sent for Frank at once and confronted him with what he had learned.

"I've told you several times, Frank, to forget this nonsense, but evidently you don't propose to take my advice." Oatman made no effort to conceal his perturbation. "Why you, a brilliant young lawyer, just getting yourself established, should endanger your practice by such folly is beyond me. Before people go to a lawyer, the one thing they want to know is that he's got his feet on the ground and is not inclined to go off half-cocked on such stuff as this. Before you took this step, why didn't you come to me?"

"Frankly, because I know how you feel about what you call my nonsense. There's oil out there, Charlie. I know it." Grimwood was trying to be patient with him. He didn't intend to back down, however. "It could be the making of Boulder City and all of us."

"Hunh!" Oatman snorted sarcastically. "Just try to get people to believe it!"

In his anger, he longed to tell Grimwood that he could forget this oil well business once and for all or consider himself no longer the First National's legal counsel. But he had only to think of Tony to realize that he didn't dare to issue such an ultimatum as that. Where she was concerned, Frank Grimwood was his best defense against Rocky Jeanette. Break with him, and there was no telling what might happen.

"Somebody's been encouraging you, Frank," he snapped. "Who is it? Jeanette?"

"Rocky's interested," Frank acknowledged.

"I knew it!" Oatman banged his desk with his fist for greater emphasis. "I suppose he's filled you full of hot air about organizing a company to put down a well! Is that it?"

His tone suggested that he had caught a small boy with his finger in the jam pot. Grimwood met it with a mirthless smile.

"I prefer," he said pointedly, "to have Rocky answer that question for himself. But I can tell you, Charlie, I'm not dropping this oil matter. I'm indebted to you for many favors. I hope never to forget that. On the other hand, I have too much faith in Mustard Valley to turn my back on it. I know I'd always regret it if I did."

Oatman nodded. "If that is the way you feel, it doesn't leave anything further to be said."

On leaving the bank, Grimwood went to Rocky's office at once and acquainted him with the situation. Rocky refused to get excited.

"I'll drop in and have a talk with him," he said.

"The sooner the better, I guess. The bank's closed, but he'll be there."

Frank shook his head pessimistically.

"You might just as well save your breath. Our guns are spiked as far as he's concerned."

"Not my guns," said Rocky. His gray eyes were frosty as he reached for his hat. "Charlie Oatman will listen to me."

12

INWARDLY SEETHING, CHARLIE OATMAN SAT ALONE in the bank, his thoughts running in circles. Not knowing how far Frank and Rocky had gone with their plans, he imagined the worst. What he could do about it, he didn't know; his hands were tied as far as Frank Grimwood was concerned; and when it came to Rocky, his sense of frustration was so complete that he could only wince and shake his head at the hopelessness of what he saw before him.

"It was a long time coming," he told himself, "but I knew the crook in him would show up. He's just using Frank; the whole thing is a trick so he can get his hands on some easy money."

A cold chill ran down his spine, when it occurred to him that, sooner or later, he would be asked to contribute to this swindle.

"I won't have any choice about it," he thought. "He'll tighten the screws and force me to buy his worthless stock. When he's got me loaded up, he'll publicize it and use it as his best argument to get a hundred others to hand over their money."

He went even further in his thoughts. When Rocky had grabbed everything in sight, he'd disappear between darkness and dawn, leaving his bilked stockholders and those who had led them into the fiasco to take the consequences.

There was something in the thought that made Oatman sit up. Wasn't that what he wanted—to be rid of the man? Rocky would never be able to show his face in Boulder City again. Why not let him get away with this fake? No matter what it cost, it would be worth the price.

"No!" he muttered. "I won't drag my friends down to save my skin! I'll stall him off and smash this bubble before anyone gets hurt!"

He was at the point of leaving the bank for Rocky's office, when he saw the latter approaching the door. He let him in at once.

"I figured we better have a little talk," said Rocky. "I just left Frank. He told me what you'd had to say."

"Then it won't be necessary for me to repeat it to you," Oatman snapped, leading the way to his desk. "I knew you were a crook, Jeanette, and I expected you to pull something like this. Take it from me, you won't get away with this swindle."

"That's pretty strong talk," Rocky returned easily, making himself comfortable in a chair. "Call this oil well proposition a gamble, and I'll agree with you; but there's no swindle about it."

"Don't try to tell me anything of the sort," Charlie whipped out. "Frank Grimwood trusts you implicitly;

123

you can pull the wool over his eyes, but you can't do it with me. You'll get your hands on the money that's turned in for stock and fly the coop."

Rocky's laugh had a distinctly unpleasant edge.

"You're putting ideas in my head, Charlie. If I played it that way, it would be right up your alley, wouldn't it?"

"No," Oatman replied, shaking his head slowly, "I've had that out with myself. As much as I'd like to see the last of you, I'm not helping you to get away with this scheme. You're not so smart I can't keep a step ahead of you. It isn't only the stock you hope to shove off on me that you're counting on; I'm to be the decoy to bring the other suckers in. I won't stand for it, Jeanette, no matter what it costs me. You crack your whip, and I'll crack mine."

Rocky began to realize that swinging him into line was going to be more difficult than he had anticipated.

"You can upset the apple-cart if you don't mind paying the price. It'll be stiff. This deal is on the level. You like to talk about what you've done for this town. If we bring in oil, Boulder City will really be put on the map. It'll make millionaires of you and me and a lot of others. Louie Abramson is in with us, and so is Mrs. Warren. They're not crazy. From the first time Frank mentioned it, you've taken the pig-headed stand that there couldn't be oil in the Blue Rock. You don't know anything about it; it may turn out to be one of the richest fields in the country."

He paused to regard Oatman with a pitying glance.

"I've got my heart set on this proposition," he said thinly. "Believe me, Charlie, if you do anything to kill it, I'll go to the mat with you. If you figure it's worth your while to throw everything away just to stop me, go to it."

Oatman sat there, his face drawn and his eyes never still. Throwing the names of Louie Abramson and Rita Warren at him had had a very sobering effect. They were two of the First National's biggest depositors.

"What do you mean, telling me Louis and Mrs. Warren are in this thing with you?"

"Just that. Louie is the secretary and treasurer of the company. Mrs. Warren is taking a couple of thousand dollars' worth of stock. They know it's a gamble. That's the way we're going to sell the deal; no big promises. Whoever comes in, comes in with his eyes open."

Without being interrupted, he talked for fifteen minutes. Gradually he saw Charlie Oatman's stubborn resistance fade. Louie Abramson was to handle the money. That fact weighed heavily with Oatman. Louie could be trusted.

"Am I to understand that nothing is to be said about this business until the meeting, Thursday noon?" he asked.

"Unless this surveyor and his rodman show up before then, and it isn't likely they will." Rocky's grin was working again. "I thought you'd appreciate the honor of being the one to break the news. You're a good speaker. Whatever remarks you care to make will be all right with us. Naturally, we'd like to set things off with a bang."

Oatman nodded woodenly.

"I imagine I know what is required . . . How much do you expect me to put into the company?"

Rocky spread his hands and said, "That's up to you." He felt he could afford to be generous.

"Not over three or four thousand," said Oatman. "That's as strong as I can go."

"Fine," Rocky told him. "We'll put this thing over the top in a couple of weeks. I know this is your town, Charlie, and it's mine, too. If we can pull together a little, it won't be any flag stop when we get through."

Grimwood was waiting for him, when he got back to the office. Rocky was in high spirits.

"Forget the grin," said Frank. "You don't have to put on an act for me. You got your ears slapped down, didn't you?"

"I did not. Everything's okay. Oatman's coming in for three or four thousand, and he's going to make the announcement and give us a boost at the club on Thursday."

"You don't mean it!" It was incredible to Grimwood. "How in heaven did you work it?"

Rocky answered with a characteristic shrug.

"I talked fast," he said. "Charlie Oatman likes to huff and puff but if you stay with him he can be handled. If that surveyor shows up before Thursday, I'll run him out of town!"

It happened that when Thursday noon came the formation of the Blue Rock Oil Company was still a closely guarded secret.

"No guest speaker today," Louis Abramson informed Rocky, just before they sat down. "Ty asked Charlie how come, and Charlie told him he had an important announcement to make that was of such great local interest that he thought there wouldn't be time for a speaker. Sounds good, eh?"

"Sure does," Rocky agreed. "I'll pass the word along to Frank."

After the coffee was served, Oatman rapped for attention.

"I believe that in the years to come, we'll look back on this meeting as a memorable occasion," he began. "Not so long ago, there wasn't a foot of paved street in Boulder City. There was a plank sidewalk on one side of Bridger Street, and it was the only one in town. The only street lights were at the bank corner. It was the regular thing for a bunch of cowboys to shoot them out every Saturday night. I'm not accusing anyone present of engaging in the practice."

He meant this to win a laugh and he was not disappointed.

"The bank stood where it's located now," he continued. "It was a small sheet iron building with a brick front in those days. There wasn't a two-story building in town. Boulder City has come a long way since then. The changes have been great. There's no need to recount them; you are as familiar with them as I. But, in view of the news I have for you today, I think I am justified in saying that what has been accomplished is only the beginning."

He went on to point out that if Boulder City was to continue to grow and its prosperity increase, they could not look to the cattle business to accomplish it. The range would not support more cattle than were on it now. The mines in the Dry Creek Mountains could not be expected to supply the added increment. Having pointed out those pertinent facts, he was ready to give his listeners the magic word "oil." Oil on the Blue Rock! In Mustard Valley!

A company was being formed. He named those behind it. The stock was to be offered at a dollar a share. Fifty thousand dollars had to be subscribed. He mentioned his own commitment for three thousand, and Rita Warren's subscription. After stressing the fact that the venture was a pure gamble, that no guarantees or glittering promises could be made, he proceeded to paint a glowing picture of what the discovery of oil would mean to each and everyone present. He urged them to get behind the company, to support it in every way possible.

"Not only as a matter of civic pride," said he. "If the company strikes oil, the returns will be tremendous. If they bring in a dry well, we won't get a penny back. It's win or lose all. Frank Grimwood is convinced there's oil in Mustard Valley. When a man will stick to his convictions the way he has, and not be turned aside by the doubting Thomases—and I was one of them—and then finds evidence to support his claims, you've got to believe him. I want Frank to address you."

Grimwood told them what he found in the valley and used a scientific yardstick to substantiate his argument. His unquestionable sincerity carried conviction.

Rocky made a few remarks, but it was little Louis Abramson who got the laughter and the cheers. Before he sat down, Louie said:

"Nobody's ever been able to follow me around by

the money I've thrown away. If this thing is good enough for me, it ought to be good enough for you. I'm in for a thousand bucks. That speaks for itself, don't it? You boys get ready; I'll be around to see you."

Before the meeting adjourned, over half of the fifty thousand had been subscribed. Leaving the hotel with Rocky, Grimwood was openly elated. Beneath the surface Rocky was no less enthused.

"Charlie certainly came through for us," said Frank.

Rocky just nodded. He didn't believe for a moment that Oatman had any faith in the company; he had only buckled under to save himself.

"I won't have to worry about him any more," Rocky thought. "No matter what comes up, he'll never cross me."

Now that there was no longer any need for secrecy, Grimwood was anxious to be the first to tell Tony the news. He had to run out to the lake to find her. She was in the water, when he arrived. He waved her in and she sat on the dock with him.

"That's wonderful news!" she said. "If I don't seem as surprised as you expected, it's because I surmised it would be something of this sort. You didn't have a word to say about what took you to Cheyenne. I thought that a pretty good tip."

Grimwood's smile broadened.

"I didn't think I was fooling you very much. That's why I didn't want you to guess. This is a dream come true for me. I'm still dazed over your father's change of mind. Did you have anything to do with it, Tony?"

"Not a thing, Frank! Dad never mentioned the matter to me. He's deep; you never know what he's going to do . . . When will you get started?"

"Early this fall. I'll go East to engage a contractor." He grew sober. "I owe everything to Rocky. He knows how to whip people into line and get what he wants. But for him, I'd still be just talking oil and getting nowhere. I don't suppose I should say it, but to see how he pushes ahead scares me sometimes. He doesn't let anything stand in his way."

It shocked Tony to have him echo a thought that she had been trying to put out of her mind for days. The long curve was gone from her lips as she looked away.

"You're the balance wheel he needs, Frank; you'll be good for him and he'll be good for you. The two of you will go a long way together."

He waited for her to dress, and they drove into town. The *Mercury* was off the press. Most of its front page was devoted to the oil project. After reading the story from beginning to end, Tony suggested that the dinner party she had mentioned be arranged for the following evening.

"I'll get word to Rita in the morning," she said. "We can find Rocky now. The four of us will have dinner and spend the rest of the evening in the studio. We have something to celebrate now."

In the morning, the partners rented the vacant storeroom for a month. After the windows had been washed and the place cleaned up, they moved in a desk and chairs. Louie sent over the young man who made his display cards. Rocky told him what was wanted.

Don Pierce, the publisher of the *Mercury*, came in.

"I see you're going right ahead," he observed. "When are you opening up for business?"

"We're open right now," Rocky replied. "We ain't turning down no one. Officially, I guess it will be Monday before we open shop. We want about fifty copies of yesterday's paper, Don. We're going to put a display in the window. It won't hurt to paste yesterday's front page on the glass."

During the day, a stream of well-wishers, many of them members of the Business Men's Club, dropped in. When five o'clock came, Grimwood suggested that they lock up.

"We're due at Tony's at seven. I've talked so much I'm hoarse."

He was the first of her guests to arrive. Rita and Rocky came together, in one of her carriages.

Rita was in a gay mood. She was leaving on Monday, for Denver. It had been a busy day for the Blue Rock Oil Company. Further commitments, totaling over ten thousand dollars, had been made. Rita spoke enthusiastically of the success Rocky and Frank were having, and, if she had had her way, would have made it the real reason for the four of them getting together.

Rocky took a hand before it went too far.

"I've had all the oil I can stand for today," he protested banteringly. "I'm looking forward to getting back to your studio, Tony, and seeing that painting."

Tony thanked him with her eyes.

"Of course!" Rita exclaimed. "I know it will be a treat."

She knew she had been rebuffed but she couldn't quite decide whether it had been intentional.

Mr. and Mrs. Oatman had gone to the hotel for dinner, leaving the house to Tony and her guests. Tony had herself well in hand and more than held her own with Rita.

Grimwood had never known her to be so vivacious. Rocky noticed, too, and all through dinner he was aware of how often Frank got her attention. Nor did he miss the adroitness with which she managed to couple him with Rita. His ego was such that he refused to believe it was anything other than a game to make him understand how little he meant to her.

After dinner, they went back to Tony's comfortable log studio, at the rear of the spacious yard. Without ceremony, she invited them to view The Cross Pull. Grimwood called it the best thing she had ever done. Rita was full of praise. It was Rocky, however, who was most impressed.

"It's wonderful," he declared, as he sat studying it. He shook his head at some secret thought. "The whole story's there, Tony. I'd like to own that picture; and I will some day if this oil thing comes through."

"What are you asking for it?" Rita inquired.

The question came so quickly that Tony surmised that it was Rita's intention to purchase the painting for Rocky.

"I haven't put a price on it," Tony answered carelessly. "Of course, I want to show it before I sell it."

No more was said about it. They sat around for an hour, admiring the Indian furnishings and a number of Tony's sketches. She played the guitar rather well. At Frank's urging she played and they sang. It was plain, old-fashioned fun, but even Rita got into the spirit of it.

When the party broke up, Rocky left with her. Frank lingered for a few minutes with Tony.

"It was a grand evening," he said, proudly. "Rita really went for it. As for Rocky, I'm sure he enjoyed it."

Tony, rearranging the chairs, had her back to him. "I hope so," she said, her smile inscrutable.

A surveyor and a rodman arrived from Cheyenne on Saturday morning. Grimwood left for the desert with them within the hour. It was after midnight when they returned to town, and the partners did not get together until Sunday breakfast.

"Everything went all right," Frank replied to Rocky's question about what had been done. "I brought in a lot of junk for the window display. I'll go down to the store this morning and fix things up. You're going out to the ranch, I understand."

"Rita's expecting me," said Rocky. "She's leaving on the morning train."

"I don't know why I don't go with her," Frank spoke up. "We'll be company for each other as far as Cheyenne. I can make it. Marion will come down and finish typing the papers today if I ask her. About an hour's work."

"Do it, by all means," Rocky urged. "It's a long ride to Cheyenne. Rita will be glad to have you for company."

They talked as they ate. After breakfast Rocky walked around the corner to the livery barn to hire a team and rig and set off for the Spanish Ranch, where he arrived in time to catch the Sunday morning workouts. Seated on the rail with Rita, they clocked the younger Warren horses as the exercise boys put them through their paces.

It was the beginning of a pleasant and exciting day for Rocky. After touring the stables and visiting old Hamilcar, the sire of most of the Warren string, they returned to the house for lunch.

Rita was glad to learn that Frank would be on the train with her as far as Cheyenne. It occurred to her, however, that with the two of them away Rocky would be left with Tony. Though she realized that with the oil company in its formative stage his answer would have to be no, she urged him again to run down to Denver.

"There's nothing I'd like better," he told her, "but I can't get away now. We'll make it some other time."

She had to be content with that.

Having disposed of Joe Bucktoe had won Rocky the esteem of the help. The well-organized staff, from old Posie and Crissy down to the newest boy on the place, lost no opportunity to show him their admiration. It touched off something in Rocky. This was as near as he had ever come to luxury. He wanted more of it, to have and to hold for his own. Life here with Rita would be very pleasant, he told himself. He didn't anticipate any difficulty in his conquest of her.

Rita, for her part, didn't bother to wonder what was running through his mind. She meant to have him, but she was too experienced to make the mistake of immediate surrender. She had him interested, but she meant to keep him dangling until she was sure of him.

Rocky was at the depot to see her and Frank off, next morning. Early as it was, he went to the store as soon as the train had pulled out.

The promotion signs and the specimens Frank had brought in were in the window, attractively arranged.

Judge Bonfils was the first to drop in. He told Rocky to put him down for a modest five hundred dollars. He mentioned his brothers and asked if they had come in.

"We hooked Sam, Judge," Rocky told him. "We'll go after Lee and Bert if they ever hit town."

The Judge laughed. "Maybe they're staying away on purpose. About fifteen years ago they let a lightning-rod salesman sell them a set of rods for one of the barns. It burned down the next week, and they haven't taken a chance on anything since."

There were other visitors as the morning wore on, and there was an ever-changing group examining the display in the window. The subscription list continued to grow. Whether the request was for a few shares or many, Rocky was happy to receive it. The excitement of it took charge of him and he forgot all about his insurance business.

Louie Abramson popped in to see how things were going. Rocky showed him the list.

"We're doing all right," Louie declared. "I got a couple fellas lined up. I'll bring them in later."

He'd been gone only a few minutes, when Tony passed. She waved to him and would have gone on had he not called her in.

"You're busy, Rocky. I can just feel the excitement in here. You haven't any time for me this morning."

"I've always got time for you, Tony." And then, quickly, "You seldom get downtown in the morning. How come this morning?"

"I've had wonderful news, Rocky. I've been commissioned to do two historical things for the Wyoming exhibit at the World's Fair. I submitted the sketches months ago and just got word this morning. I rushed down to get off a letter of acceptance. Isn't it grand?"

"It's no more than you deserve." His tone was sober. He meant what he was saying, for once. "A thousand years from now folks can look at your paintings and see what things were like around here in our time."

Pop Singer, the town marshal, strolled in and sat down. He had been in once before. He continued to sit around after Tony left. He loved to talk, and he was apparently just killing time. Somehow, Rocky got the feeling Pop was watching the door. Certainly his glance strayed that way every few seconds.

Rocky got busy and Pop walked out. He hadn't been gone long before Ty Roberts came in. He sat around, too. He had a gun on his hip, and he usually didn't when he was in town.

Rocky began to tighten up. He could feel the alertness that lurked beneath Ty's calm demeanor. Finally, Rocky couldn't stand it any longer.

"What's up?" he demanded. "Pop's been in here a couple times, and now you show up. If you've got anything on your mind, let's have it."

"Say, yo're a little jittery, ain't you?" Ty demanded,

surprised at Rocky's tone. "Calm down; ain't nothin' wrong so far."

"What do you mean?" Rocky was still puzzled.

"Jim Bucktoe, Joe's brother, hit town this mornin'. He ain't likkerin' up and he ain't blowin' off his mouth, but Pop and I got the idea that mebbe he came in lookin' to square accounts with you. You killed his brother. We figgered we'd hang around, just in case. If Jim was makin' any war talk, we'd lock him up. But he ain't sayin' a thing . . . You keep yore eyes open, Rocky. I'll just walk across the street and hang around till Pop gits back."

Rocky thanked him. For once he forgot to grin. He wasn't taking the warning lightly. Being unarmed, he began looking for something that he could use for a weapon with which to defend himself. A small hammer was the best thing he could find. He tossed it aside in disgust.

"A lot of good that would be," he thought. "Everything going swell, and this has got to come up!"

He could see Ty across the street. Fifteen minutes later the sheriff was still there. Rocky's tension began to fad. A prospective stockholder came in. The usual questions and answers followed. It was another sale. Only fifty shares this time. With the man's departure, Rocky looked up to find a short, chunky Indian gazing at the display in the window. Their eyes met through the glass. The Indian moved to the door then, and when he stepped inside, his right hand was in his pocket.

Rocky backed away and put a desk between them.

The Indian took another hesitant step and stopped,

a hollow grin of embarrassment on his round face. The next moment, Ty's broad shoulders filled the doorway.

"All right, Jim!" he ground out. "What is it?"

The Indian turned to him. "Oil," he said. His hand came out of his pocket, clutching a crumpled five-dollar bill. "Me buy oil."

"You mean you want to buy stock in the company?" Ty demanded, his amazement choking him.

"Yeh. Plenty time I see oil in Mustard Valley."

Ty expelled the air from his lungs with a noisy whoosh.

"Wal, I'll be damned!" he exploded. "That takes the cake! Pop and me was gittin' all spooked up for nothin'!"

13

By the first of October, the sixteen-mule teams and the freighting wagons had ground out a passable road to Mustard Valley. Of a Sunday, it had become quite the thing for the townspeople, most of them stockholders, to drive out to watch the drilling. Tony had been out several times. Rita was there oftener.

A barn with a galvanized iron roof, and still open at the sides, as well as half-a-dozen small cabins, had been erected on the property. Grimwood used one of the cabins for the company's field headquarters and the personal accommodation of Rocky and himself.

Frank had turned over his law practice to Gene Robbins temporarily, so that he might spend all his time in camp. The storeroom in town, from which the company had been promoted, had become the permanent office, with Rocky in charge of the business at that end and shuttling back and forth between town and the valley three and four times a week.

Organizing the freighting had been an arduous

chore. Rocky had supervised it from the first and managed to keep supplies and material rolling. The worst of that was over. He still had two carloads of thirty-foot lengths of five-and-five-eighths-inch casing on a siding in the Wyoming & Western yard, but he was so far ahead of the drillers that he began to spend more and more of his time in the field. The bit was cutting ever deeper into the surface strata and once he got on the platform and heard it thudding into the rock, the creaking of the walking-beam and the groaning of the bull-wheel filling his ears, he couldn't tear himself away.

Every Sunday brought Louie Abramson out from town. It was the only day he could get away from the store. He had come into the company believing he would do well to break even. When Charlie Oatman had given it his enthusiastic endorsement, Louie had thought better of his investment. But even then he regarded it as no more than a good gamble that wasn't going to hurt anyone very much if it ended in failure. Of late, however, oil fever began to grip him, too. He had never had any great interest in anything that didn't begin and end with the store. Now he complained to Frank and Rocky over the fact that Sunday was the only day he had free.

"This thing gets into your blood," he confessed. "I'm getting so I can't sleep. Getty tells me everything still looks good. No sign of trouble ahead, eh?"

"Not according to what the bailer brings up," said Grimwood. "We ought to be about through the shale and getting into sandstone. If we strike any real trouble, it won't be for a couple weeks. We're not down far enough for that."

"They're bringing the bailer up now," Rocky reported from the doorway. "Let's see what they've got."

The bailer was swung around to the waste trough and emptied itself when it struck bottom. Grimwood and John Getty, the contractor, examined the detritus carefully.

"Shale, nothing else," said Getty. He found a piece containing a small fossil. After wiping it off on his overalls, he handed it to Frank, saying, "Souvenir for you." With his hand, he stirred the mixture of muck and oily water that had just been brought up and then tested its viscosity by rubbing thumb and forefinger together. "Getting heavier. Not a bad sign. Of course, only the bit will show if there's oil."

It was one of his favorite sayings. He and Frank's father had been close friends for years. That alone had made it possible to persuade him to come to Wyoming. A better man for the job couldn't have been found. He was critical in his judgments and not given to loose optimism. On being shown over the property for the first time and having the pool of seepage and the oil-impregnated sandstone outcroppings shown him, he had declared the prospects decidedly favorable, only to add his now familiar, "But only the bit will show if there's oil." But he was impressed, and had continued to be. Coming from a man who knew his business, and guarded his enthusiasm so carefully, it had further encouraged the partners.

This Sunday passed, as the others preceeding it had,

without one of the Blue Rock Oil Company's most important stockholders putting in an appearance. Frank and Louie couldn't understand why Charlie Oatman never found time to come out. It wasn't any mystery to Rocky.

"Oatman ain't too busy," he told himself. "He'd like to see what we're doing, but he's staying away because he's sure the well is going to be a bust."

If he had included Oatman's bitter hatred of himself, he would have been close to the truth. Like the proverbial horse of the familiar adage, Oatman had been led to the water but he wasn't going to be made to drink. He kept himself informed on how the work was progressing. Almost every day, someone who had just returned from Mustard Valley, came into the bank and supplied him with the latest details.

Considering his position, the keen interest he expressed in the operations was understandable. For him to have done otherwise would have excited suspicion. Forestalling the inevitable question, he was always ready with a plausible excuse for his own non-appearance.

Like a condemned man, watching the clock as he awaited his doom, Oatman kept the score on the drilling. Every foot the drill went down was another second ticked away for him, bringing the disastrous conclusion ever nearer.

He spent hours contemplating what his position would be when the bubble burst and men like Joe Evans, Ty Roberts, the Judge and several hundred others, were brought face to face with the fact that the money they had invested in the company was irretrievably lost. Being human beings, they would very likely forget that they had been told they were taking a gamble, and remember only that he had sponsored the company. He had invested his money. That would be a mitigating factor. Even so, he would not be able to escape the storm completely; the best he could hope for was to weather it and then try to rebuild his battered fences.

When the hour of disillusionment came, where would Rocky stand? Charlie dwelt long and intently on that question. The Blue Rock Oil Company was his idea; more than anyone else, he was responsible for the folly in which Boulder City was indulging.

"He'll have a hard row to hoe around here," Oatman told himself. "He's dealing with men who are hard losers. They'll let him know how they feel."

Though the past weeks had been trying ones for him, it was a great comfort to notice how little Tony was seeing of Rocky. Charlie Oatman knew it wasn't due solely to the fact that Rocky was busy; during the several weeks that Mrs. Warren and Frank had been away, he had not been to the house once. Tony had been working feverishly, and on finishing the pictures for the Wyoming exhibit, had turned at once to doing several things she wanted to take to San Francisco, along with The Cross Pull.

Gossip had begun to couple Rocky with Rita. She had returned in triumph from Denver and San Antonio. Rocky had been at the depot to meet her. On his frequent trips back and forth to Mustard Valley, he never failed to spend an hour or two at the Spanish Ranch.

Charlie was only too willing to accept at their face value the inferences being made. Mrs. Warren was a rich and attractive young widow. Knowing Rocky, he didn't doubt what his intentions were concerning her. It was a regrettable situation to him, for he had a high regard for Rita Warren. His regret, however, ran a bad second to his relief respecting Tony's diminished interest in the man.

Difficult as he knew his own position was going to be after the debacle, he promised himself that he would have to do something for Frank Grimwood. With this oil madness out of his mind, Frank would settle down to business. After a year or two, he could step into politics.

He didn't hold Frank's defiance against him. The boy had fallen under Rocky Jeanette's influence; that had been his great mistake. He himself was, in part, responsible for this miserable mess, but only to a minor degree. By and large, Frank would make a satisfactory son-in-law. It had always been one of Charlie's fears that Tony would bring home a husband who would be an everlasting disappointment to him.

Rita arranged a dinner party early in the week. Tony begged off immediately. It brought Rita to the studio.

"You can't be so busy it's impossible for you to take an evening off," she argued. "I don't see anything of you any more. You've been cooping yourself up in here day after day. It's beginning to tell on you, Tony. You're thin."

"A little," Tony admitted lightly. "I'll get it back

in California. I want to get away next Sunday if possible."

Four paintings were already boxed for shipment.

"I didn't know you were leaving," said Rita. "Is this something that came up unexpectedly?"

"No, I've been going down every year for the annual California Oil and Water-color Show. I want to take this one down with me." She indicated the picture on the easel. "I've three or four days' work to do."

"I'm sorry you can't make it," Rita gave in at last. "Rocky is coming. Frank promised that he would come in. Of course, he won't make the effort if you're not to be there."

"That's sweet of Frank to be as faithful as that," Tony remarked, thinking that Rita had on too much make-up. "I told him, when I was out in the valley two weeks ago, that I'd be going down about the ninth of the month. He's undoubtedly forgotten; he and Rocky are so busy."

Rocky was in town that afternoon. Rita saw him and told him the party was off, and why. After she had left for the ranch, he made a sudden decision. Ten minutes later, he opened the studio door. Tony was busy at the easel.

"Well, this is unexpected!" she exclaimed, turning to him.

"Can I come in?" he asked.

"Of course. I don't know whether you can find a chair. Things are in a mess."

"You're leaving, I understand," he said, his whole attention fixed on her.

"You must have seen Rita."

"Yeh . . . What were you going to do—leave without saying good-by to anyone?"

"Anyone?" she queried, her bantering tone stabbing him.

"Well, to me, then," he muttered soberly.

Tony laughed. "You make it sound important."

Something electric had touched the air with his coming. He pulled up a chair. Straddling it, he placed his elbows on the back and gazed at her approvingly.

"I haven't seen you in weeks, Tony. I missed you the last time, when you drove out with the Taylors."

"I've been right here," she said, cleaning a brush with greater care than was necessary. "You've been terribly busy, I know."

"It wasn't being busy that kept me away." He got up and pushed the chair out of his way. "I put the brakes on and kept away from you because I knew I had to. I thought I could lick this thing."

He reached out suddenly and caught her hands.

"Tony, let's quit kidding ourselves!"

She broke away as he tried to draw her into his arms.

"Not that . . . no!" she protested.

She stood there for a moment, getting hold of herself, her breasts rising and falling with her deep, excited breathing.

"There was a time, Rocky, when I might have been foolish enough to let you sweep me off my feet . . . Those moments pass, and when they're gone, you wonder that you could have thought of throwing everything away on a mad impulse . . . I'm Frank's girl. Remember?"

"You are if he can hold you." Unconsciously, Rocky pulled down the corners of his mouth, and his eyes were grim in his hard, flat face. "I never have pretended to be a gentleman; when I see something I want, I take it if I can get it."

Tony winced. "I wish you hadn't said that."

"What difference can it make now? It's true. I knew I shouldn't have come here today; I've gone too far in another direction for it to do me any good. Talk about throwing everything away! I thought I was being smart, and I've made the biggest mistake of my life. But you know how I feel, and I'm glad you do. That's all I've got to say."

He didn't stay long. On leaving, he said, "Where are you going to be in San Francisco?"

"At the St. Francis . . . Why do you ask?"

"Maybe I'll send you a postcard," he growled sarcastically as he slammed out of the studio.

Tony was satisfied to let him go. She didn't know whether she wanted to cry or laugh. She did neither. She had humbled him, and that's what she had been wanting to do for weeks. She didn't doubt that he was as ruthless and bereft of honor as he claimed to be. It didn't frighten her.

"Why should it?" she asked herself. "He means nothing to me. This ended any chance that he might."

She was glad it was over and done with, and doubly glad she had Frank.

"If he were here now," she thought, "and asked me to be his wife, I'd marry him in a minute."

Before she left for the coast, Frank came in and spent the evening with her. He looked tired. The strain he was under was telling on him. It worried her.

"You're not getting rest enough, Frank. You can't be up day and night."

"I know it," he agreed. "I turn in, and if the drill misses a beat, I've got to get out and see what's wrong. The work's going ahead satisfactorily. We ran into a hard conglomerate this morning. Getty isn't worried; he says we'll break through it. But it slows things up for the present. You'll be home long before we're ready to shoot the well. Of course, we may hit a gusher that'll blow everything sky high before we shoot." He laughed at the possibility. "That'd upset our calculations most pleasantly."

"You're as confident as ever, Frank?"

"Oh, sure! I don't see how we can miss. Coming across the desert this afternoon, I promised myself that the first thing I'll do after we bring the well in will be to buy the finest diamond ring in this town and ask you to let me put it on your finger. When I first mentioned oil in the Blue Rock, you encouraged me, and you were the only one who did. I know Rocky wouldn't have got interested but for you. If I hit the jack-pot, I'll owe it all to you."

Tony's head was on his shoulder. "I guess you know what my answer will be," she murmured, without looking up. "It'll be the same if you don't strike oil."

Tony had not been gone more than a week, when Rocky drove into camp. After assuring himself that everything was going smoothly, he asked if Grimwood could get along without him for a few days.

"I don't know why not," Frank told him. "If anything unexpected comes up at the office, I can run into town and take care of it."

Rocky explained that one of the insurance companies he represented was calling its agents into the home office, at Sacramento, for its annual convention. It was his biggest account, he said.

Grimwood did not for a moment question the truthfulness of the story.

"Go ahead," he said. "Get back when you can."

Rocky let it go at that. For the past few days he had been in a savage mood, his preoccupation so intense that it had not escaped Rita's notice. She surmised that something in connection with the oil company was responsible. She had tried to break through it, even suggesting that if they were running out of funds, she might be able to do something about it.

Rocky had brushed it off, and not too gently either. Today, when he stopped to tell her he was going to the convention, her suspicions instantly took another direction. Tony was in California. She was shrewd enough not to mention it, but on the train that carried Rocky to the Coast, there were several letters from her to friends in San Francisco.

Her letters were answered in due course, and the information they held was so infuriating that she made no effort to contain herself. Rocky's deceit, she might have forgiven; but in her jealous rage, she found the cruelest blow in the fact that he held her cheaply, and for that there was no forgiveness.

Determined to avenge the indignity he had offered her, she had a team harnessed and drove to Mustard Valley.

Grimwood realized at once that something was wrong.

"You're upset, Rita," he said anxiously. "I hope it isn't bad news."

"Frank—I think it's about time someone opened your eyes."

His head went up, and he gazed at her, more puzzled than ever.

"I don't get you—"

"Rocky," she informed him.

"Rocky?"

"He lied to you. He isn't in Sacramento. He went straight to San Francisco to be near Tony. I have friends in the city. They've written. Rocky and Tony are out dining and dancing every night."

Grimwood's fingers tightened on the buggy wheel as he steadied himself.

"I'd trust Tony anywhere," he declared, his throat tight. "Dining and dancing sounds like innocent fun."

"It may be innocent enough on Tony's part. Rocky doesn't intend it to be innocent." Rita had thrown discretion to the winds. "When I first met him, I realized that he was reaching out for her. You were his friend, but that didn't matter to him. He doesn't let anything stand in his way."

Frank winced. His own words were being tossed back at him now.

"He accepted my favors and made me believe I meant something to him," Rita rushed on, her dark eyes flashing angrily. "He was only using me; and I despise him for it!"

Her voice broke, and she paused to catch her breath.

The blood had drained away from Frank's cheeks and under its tan his face was grim. Though he was slow to anger, Rita could see his wrath rising.

"Frank—what are you going to do?"

"I don't know," he said slowly. "Nothing foolish, Rita. He lied to me. That'll take some answering. But I'm not rushing down to San Francisco. He'll be home in a day or two. I'll be in town, waiting for him."

14

DOWN IN CALIFORNIA ROCKY WAS NOT CONCERNED about hurrying back to Wyoming. He had threatened to leave, but that was done only in the hope of bringing Tony to terms. To his complete annoyance, she had urged him to go. Sulking, he had stayed away from her for two days. They had dined and danced and done the theaters, but she had always been in command, and he had failed dismally in his plans to sweep her off her feet. After almost a week of it, they had quarreled.

This afternoon, however, when she stepped out of the Grant Avenue gallery, where her paintings were being exhibited, she found Rocky waiting for her.

"I thought you'd left town," she said, attempting to convey by her tone that it meant little to her, one way or the other.

"Don't tell me anything like that," he countered, with a grin. "You knew I wouldn't go without saying good-by. I've been trying to put you out of my mind—

trying to turn to other things." With characteristic suddenness, he was sober and in great earnest. "That didn't get me anywhere." He shook his head. "You were right; it was crazy of me to show up here in Frisco and make a big play for you. But if a guy wants something so bad he can't think straight, you shouldn't hold it against him."

Tony smiled and took his arm. "I don't hold anything against you, Rocky. You can walk me over to my hotel if you like. And thanks for seeing it my way; I knew you would if you sat down and thought it over."

"This is more like it," he said, happily, as they swung along the avenue. "You were pretty rough on me the other night . . . Oh, sure, I had it coming. I sat in the park all morning, thinking about you and me. I've got to be heading back to Wyoming. I'll be pulling out in the morning."

"Again?" Tony queried, her smile challenging.

"I mean it this time. I figured if you'd see me again, we could have dinner together out at the Cliff House. I took a chance and rented a rig . . . What do you say, Tony? You don't have to be afraid of any more nonsense out of me."

She hesitated but she knew she wouldn't say no. It secretly infuriated her to find herself immediately on the defensive with him.

"It's late to drive out," she said. "The fog will be in before we get there."

"Not if we go right away. You don't have to dress. Come on, Tony, say yes," he urged. "I can be at the hotel door in ten minutes with the team. Nice high-stepping bays."

153

"All right," she gave in. "I'll need a coat; it gets cool out there in the evening."

He was waiting for her when she came down. She had changed hurriedly to a new frock that Rocky had never seen. It was very flattering. She saw his eyes warm and felt his pride in her. It was reward enough for the few extra minutes she had taken. He handed her in with a flourish and touched the team with the whip.

"This is something like it!" he declared happily, as they drove off. "You and me in a swell turnout, driving out to the Cliff House, just like a couple of swells."

In that mood, she found him irresistible. And yet, it needed only the pressure of his hand on hers, or his crooked smile and searching eyes to remind her all over again that there never could be any real or lasting armistice between them; that she could never be on safe, impersonal ground with him.

They were through Golden Gate Park and the still unimproved addition, when she said, "I took you at your word the other day. If I hadn't believed you were leaving, I wouldn't have written Frank what I did."

"Yeh?" he queried, trying not to sound interested. "What did you tell him?"

"That you were here and I had been seeing you."

He didn't like it. "You could have let him find out for himself," he said, scowling.

"Or from Rita Warren."

"Why Rita?"

"She has many friends in town. Some of them know me. If Rita is curious at all about your absence—and

I imagine she is—she's written someone. I didn't want Frank to get it that way."

"That all you said?" He told himself that he didn't care what came of Rita's spying.

"No, I mentioned that I was surprised that you could be spared, just at this time, with the two of you so busy. I said that the personal business that brought you to California must have been very pressing indeed." She saw Rocky's face go hard and flat. "I was provoked with you, Rocky, or I wouldn't have said that."

"It was catty of you," he growled softly.

"Oh, I have claws," she said lightly. "As if you didn't know." Her smile faded abruptly and she was stern with him. "That was an outrageous deception— telling him you had an insurance convention out here. I'm sure you never so much as got off the train at Sacremento . . . Did you have to lie to Frank?"

Rocky lifted his shoulders in a careless shrug. "I had to tell him something."

"You lied to him. It doesn't shame you a bit to be accused of it."

He turned to her with an impudent grin. "Tony— you keep getting me mixed up with some other guy. I've told you a dozen times I'm no gentleman. I'd sooner lie to him than hurt his feelings."

Tony shook her head reprovingly. "What an excuse! I don't know what to make of you. You have a sense of honor; you show it in a hundred ways. And yet you brush aside something like this as though it were of no importance. You do things that frighten me

—that actually make me afraid of you. I've never said it before, but I mean it, Rocky."

"Afraid of me?" he laughed. "If I hadn't promised to keep the wraps on this afternoon, I'd tell you that you're the one person in this world who'll never have any reason to be afraid of me."

There wasn't any dancing at the Cliff House but the food was excellent and, for early in the week, the restaurant was comfortably filled. The music, the soft lights and the undertone of the surf breaking on the rocks created a mood in Rocky and he became more communicative than Tony had ever known him to be. He spoke of his boyhood days in Missouri. He was farm-bred and had run away from home with a small traveling circus.

"I never went back," he told her. "My mother was gone before I left. When the old man passed away, I didn't hear about it for months. Wasn't any use going back then. The circus went bust, and I went to work for an auctioneer. I guess that's where I picked up this gift of gab. But I was a fiddlefoot; I wanted to see the country. For a couple years, I made book on the horses. I went broke at that, too. I had to turn to something in a hurry." He laughed, and his eyes were fixed on an horizon far back in his memory. "You wouldn't believe it—it was another one of those crazy things I'm always doing—but it led me to Boulder City and you."

"Don't leave me hanging in mid-air," she said banteringly. "I'm all ears. Needing money, what did you do? Hold up a train or rob a bank?"

Over the rim of his raised coffee cup, he regarded

her carefully for a moment, his eyes blank and not a muscle betraying his reaction to what he knew could be nothing more than a wild stab in the dark.

"That would have been an idea—and easier than riding bucking broncs on the rodeo circuit," he said, with an amused chuckle.

"You—riding bucking horses?"

"Yeh, and I was pretty good, too."

"I can believe it," Tony observed simply. "The first time I saw you in the saddle, I knew you could ride. How did rodeo riding ever bring you to Boulder City?"

"In a roundabout way. Down in Texas, I met a guy who was putting a show together with the idea of taking it back East to New York and other places. He asked me to throw in with him. I didn't have money, but he did. When we left Fort Worth, it took a dozen cars to haul our livestock—calves, broncs and Brahma bulls. We even hired a band and dressed 'em up in cowboy duds. We had cowgirls and all the rest of it. It was a good show. The East had never seen anything like that. We did all right. In a couple years, I was back in the chips."

"That still doesn't get you to Wyoming," Tony protested.

"That was coming," he said laughingly. "Being a sucker, I let two of my friends sell me the idea of buying a ranch and raising bucking horses for the shows. In one way and another, I soon had every dime I owned tied up in the proposition. It didn't pay off. I knew it was time for me to turn to something else again. That's when I headed for Boulder City. It doesn't add up to anything," he summed up, after a moment's pause. "But it's a good story."

"The outline is fascinating," Tony said. "I imagine if you wanted to fill in the details it would be even more exciting . . . And now you're promoting a wildcat oil well. Maybe you'll soon be in what you call the 'chips' again."

"Maybe," he replied. "You never can tell what's in the cards till they're all dealt . . . Let's get out of here, Tony, and walk along the beach for half an hour. You've got a warm coat. It'll feel good to have the wind in your face and hear the surf pounding in."

It was the custom for young couples to stroll along the beach after dinner. The fog was in, but it was a high fog and while the moon couldn't break through it, it shed an eerie radiance that gave the long strip of sand and breaking waves a ghostly beauty.

"You could paint things like this, Tony," Rocky said, as they moved along the beach.

"I doubt it," she said. "There are so many who do it so much better than I could that I shall never try. I've got my own little field and I'm going to stick with it. It isn't good for anyone to stray too often or too far from his own Reservation."

Rocky laughed. "You mean that for me as much as for yourself, don't you? I like Boulder City. It suits me fine. If I get half a break, you won't see me pulling stakes again . . . Shall we sit here on the rocks a minute? We can find a place that'll be out of the wind."

Tony knew she should say no. But she hesitated, and the decision was taken out of her hands. The fog, the booming of the surf and the lonely grandeur of the night were playing havoc with her resolves.

Just to sit there with him, not a word being spoken, was a blessed reprieve. But not for long. The desire to let herself go, if only for a moment, and be in his arms, with his kisses crushing her mouth, began to run away with her. She told herself it was sheer madness. It made her realize that it wasn't only Rocky she had to fight.

"I don't suppose we'll ever be together again like this," he said out of a long silence, a great soberness riding his words. "I've said a lot, but I've left some things unsaid. Maybe I better say them now; it ain't likely I'll ever have another chance."

"No, Rocky, please!" she pleaded. "Don't make things impossible for both of us. You've said it all, in one way or another. It's made one thing very clear to me, and I know you didn't intend that it should. I know what the talk has been about Frank and me— that we'd marry some day. It's easy to drift along with a situation like that and find yourself taking it for granted. But I was never sure in my own mind that I wanted to marry him. I am now. You've made it very clear to me."

There was a play of muscles in Rocky's cheeks that tightened his face and stamped grim lines at the corners of his mouth. "Frank's a nice guy," was his critical rejoinder. "Nothing brilliant about him. But he's steady going. No fiddlefoot like me. He'll make you a good husband. You'll always know where you stand with him." He paused, and added sardonically: "I hope you don't find it monotonous."

Tony's chin went up in indignation. "I'm not itchy-footed like you; I know what is good for me—how I want my life to go. I'll be happy with Frank Grimwood."

"Yeh," he said, with taunting sarcasm, "I can imagine how fine everything will be for you. If the oil well flops, he'll give up the law, I reckon, after your father passes away, and go into the bank. You'll go on with your painting. One day will be exactly like the next. That'll be great, won't it?" He turned on her wolfishly and pulled her into his arms. "Listen, Tony! Why kid yourself? You're not in love with Frank. A nice guy, but you're not in love with him. You're like me, you need excitement, somebody to stir you out of yourself. You don't want to know what tomorrow is going to be like till it gets here. You say you're afraid of me sometimes. Down inside of you you know you wouldn't have me any different if you could. You know I'm the man for you. I won't give you up if you marry him a dozen times!"

"Please, Rocky! Don't say such things! I refuse to listen!"

He only drew her closer and closed his ears to her pleas.

"Why have you always fought your love for me?" he demanded, his voice rough with emotion. "If it's because you figure I've gone behind Frank's back, I'll break with him—pull out of the oil company—and take my chances against him any way he wants to play it."

"No, it's too late for that, Rocky. If you love me, you'll let me go."

For answer, he tilted her face and gazed at her with savage affection. Something snapped in Tony, and she lifted her mouth for his kisses.

Later, as they drove back to town, they had little to say to each other. Finally, he said, "I don't understand you at all, Tony. I used to think I did. When you tell me that tonight hasn't changed a thing between us, I don't know what to say. I reckon it must be that I do my thinking with my heart and you do it with your head."

"Perhaps that's the way it is," was her low, tense answer. "Some things are so precious that even the memory of them hurts. When I think back to tonight, I shall tell myself that it was two other people, not really you and me, Rocky, who sat on the beach this evening and lost themselves for a few delirious moments."

Rocky gazed at her with even greater amazement. "You can say things like that and still tell me you're going to marry Grimwood?"

Tony nodded. "I've given Frank my promise. I shall keep it. I can trust myself with him, and I never could with you, darling; we're too much alike, too unpredictable, too unstable. Soon after I get home, I'll ask Father to make a formal announcement of the engagement."

He laughed bitterly. "You'll feel safe then, won't you? You won't have to face up to anything." He shook his head, his mouth grim. "Let me be the first to congratulate you."

15

A COMMITTEE, HEADED BY JINNY EVANS, HAD BEEN busy for a week arranging the Harvest Festival dance at the lake, always the last party of the year. It was usually a gala affair, with the ballroom appropriately decorated with corn stalks, the necessary pumpkins, which Chris Trinkle could be counted on to supply (his truck patch in the Squaw Creek bottoms was the only one in town) and festoons of crêpe paper.

Grimwood was in town but in no mood to attend. The morning after the party, Judge Bonfils stepped into the oil company's office, as he was passing.

"We had quite a crowd out," he told Frank. "But, as so many remarked, Mrs. Warren, Tony, you and Rocky, were conspicuous by your absence. It took the edge off the evening for me."

"I'm surprised that Rita wasn't out," said Grimwood. He hadn't expected her to attend but felt he could say nothing to Bonfils about that. It was obvious that the Judge was not aware of how matters stood between Rocky and her.

"I went out to the ranch and tried to persuade her to go, but she begged off," Bonfils explained. "Said she didn't feel up to it."

His interest in Rita Warren had long been well known. He had never shown any resentment against Rocky, when the latter had forced him to play a muted second fiddle with her. Grimwood had been puzzled by it. The friendly interest the Judge expressed in Rocky this morning seemed to be above suspicion.

"Of course," Bonfils remarked, "all everyone had to talk about was when you'd be shooting the well. How far down are you, Frank?"

"About twenty-three hundred feet."

"Then you haven't far to go—according to your previous calculations, I mean."

Grimwood nodded. He found it difficult to talk about the drilling. His interest in the well remained as great as ever, but he didn't see how Rocky and he could go on together; one of them would have to step out. He sat there brooding over it after the Judge left.

His faith in Tony remained unshaken. He refused to believe for a moment that she and Rocky were together in San Francisco by prearrangement. Even Rita, bitter as she was, had not intimated anything of that nature. Being convinced that Rocky had appeared unexpectedly and employed some falsehood to explain his presence, perhaps the very one he had used on him, Frank could find nothing reprehensible in the fact that Tony was accepting his company and attentions. After all, they were good friends; she dined and danced with him here at home. No, he repeatedly assured himself, the treachery was all on Rocky's part. Any doubt of it fled, when he received a letter from Tony, telling him Rocky had been in San Francisco and insisted on being attentive.

"Having an attractive escort to wine and dine you in San Francisco's fashionable restaurants sounds exciting, I know, but it's really been a difficult few days for me," she wrote. "I'm sure Rocky hasn't found it too pleasant, either. It may be, as you said one afternoon at the lake, that he lets nothing stand in his way. If so, he ran into the immovable object in me."

There was more. Not having seen him for a day or two, she presumed that Rocky was on his way back to Wyoming. "Knowing how busy the two of you are, I was surprised that he could be spared for even a few days," the letter continued. "The personal business he had on the Coast must have been very pressing."

"Lied to her," Grimwood muttered, reading between the lines. "The double-crossing rat made a big play and got his ears slapped down!"

He had a wire from Rocky, late that day, saying he was on the Chicago Limited and would arrive early Wednesday morning. The Limited stopped at Boulder City only to discharge passengers from the Coast. Though it was not due until a few minutes of two, Grimwood waited up.

It took Rocky another ten minutes to get up town. Seeing the lights burning in the office, he headed that way. He had only to catch a glimpse of Frank's stony face to know he had been found out.

"Well, say it!" he growled, sliding his bag into a corner.

"You lied to me." Grimwood let him have it bluntly. "You didn't have any convention in Sacramento on your mind; you went straight to San Francisco to see Tony."

"Sure I did!" Rocky flung back viciously, shoulders hunched, his brazenness an unconscious throwback to the days when he had operated with a gun in his fist. "You were keepin' cases on me, eh?"

"No, but someone else was."

"Rita?"

"Who else?"

"The snooping bitch!" Rocky snarled. "I was warned what to expect from her!"

He had risked everything in going to San Francisco. He knew that he had not only lost Tony but Rita and almost everything else as well.

"I been trying to take Tony away from you since the first time I saw her," he admitted brazenly. "I didn't want to rat on you; that's why I got mixed up with Rita Warren. I thought that'd take care of everything. But it didn't. Tony tried to show me I didn't have a chance with her. I wouldn't believe it; I figured it was just a stall. I've had a lot of experience with dames. I knew they weren't her kind. But that's what threw me; I couldn't get it through my dumb head that there was a different set of rules in her league . . . What a sap I was!"

He threw back his head and started to laugh scornfully at himself. He stopped suddenly, and his gray eyes were fierce and bitter.

165

"It's over and done with, Grimwood," he whipped out. "You can make what you please of it. I ain't apologizing for trying to beat your time. If Tony had—"

"Keep Tony out of it, if you've got any more to say!" Frank cut him off. He hauled himself to his feet and stepped around the desk, his lean jaw set at a fighting angle. "I've had a few days to think matters over. There were little things along the way that I should have noticed. But I wouldn't see them. How I could have been fool enough to think you were on the level with me is more than I'll ever know. But that's enough of that, Jeanette; we're through. Either you're going to get out of the company, or I am. I came in from camp last Friday, and I'm not going back till I know what you're going to do."

"I ain't going to do a thing!" Rocky rifled back. "I'm hanging on to my stock!"

"Hang on to it!" Grimwood's voice rose. "I can't do anything about that, but I can call a stockholders' meeting and with the proxies I can get, I can force you out and leave you nothing to say about running the company. You know I can do it, and I won't have to explain why I'm doing it."

Rocky took a step toward him, his attitude menacing.

"You better not try it!" he growled. "I won't take any pushing around from you!"

"By God, I will!" Frank retorted, anger running away with him. "On my orders, Louie has paid all the outstanding bills and notified everyone that no supplies or material of any kind are to be turned over to the company without a signed order from me."

"That was smart, wasn't it!" Rocky ripped out sarcastically. "It don't leave you money enough to meet this week's payroll! What are you going to do about that? You'll need another five thousand."

"I'll worry about that after I've got rid of you. I can raise it."

"Like hell you will! Who raised the fifty thousand you had?" Rocky's jeering laugh further infuriated Frank. "You're going to need me right down to the wire. All I got to do is sit tight to call your bluff. The company needs money, and you know I can raise it."

"You couldn't raise another nickel in this town!" The taunting sneer that contorted Rocky's face snapped the last thread of restraint in Grimwood. Careless now of what he said and wanting only to hammer that mocking face into an unrecognizable pulp, he added, "Don't kid yourself that you can blackmail it out of Charlie Oatman!"

Rocky's right hand flashed out. His fingers closed on the collar of Frank's shirt.

"What the hell do you mean?" he rapped, pulling him forward.

Grimwood slapped Rocky's hand away.

"What do you think?" he blazed as they stood toe to toe. "I'm no fool; I can put two and two together!"

Out of nowhere, he brought up his right fist and sent it crashing against Rocky's mouth. The force of it drove Rocky's head back. Blood spurted from his torn lips.

Sense went out of Rocky. In savage fury he rushed

in and drove Grimwood back against the desk. Pinning him there, he swung from his heels with right hand and left; punishing blows that hurt.

He was doing something more than trying to square accounts with Grimwood; his sense of complete frustration over the way everything had turned out for him was finding expression, and every time his fist smashed into Frank's face and made him wince, it added fresh fuel to Rocky's rage. Lady Luck had turned her back on him and played him a scurvy trick, and he wanted to get even. It was that, rather than any deep-seated hatred or ill will he bore Frank Grimwood that was driving him now.

Frank weathered that first storm and clipped Rocky on the ear with another long, whistling right. Rocky saw it coming and stepped back, trying to roll with the blow. It gave Frank his chance, and he got away from the desk quickly, flicking his left hand repeatedly to Rocky's chin and keeping him off balance.

Both had room now to move either to right or left, and they began to go to it in earnest. Like Rocky, Grimwood was venting the pent-up fury that had been tearing at him for almost a week. Physically, they were evenly matched; Frank was an inch or two the taller, with a corresponding advantage in reach, but Rocky made up for it with a catlike quickness and a pair of shoulders that had dynamite in them.

Save for the Maverick and several other nighthawk establishments, Boulder City was fast asleep. Though passersby along Bridger Street were few, that section of the street between the bank corner and the office of the Blue Rock Oil Company was never completely deserted for more than a few minutes at a time.

Two exuberant cowboys, bound for the Chinese restaurant near the depot, came along and became the first thrilled witnesses to the battle raging within. They weren't interested in the cause of the fight; it was a good fight, and it promised to continue for some time. Accordingly, word was sent back to the Maverick and before long there was a crowd at the window. Ollie Seager, the night constable, came running.

Though Ollie tried the door and found it unlocked, he didn't step in. He was charged with maintaining the peace, but he had a prejudice against interfering when two men were settling their differences by having at each other with their fists, and especially so when the combatants were such prominent citizens as Grimwood and Rocky Jeanette. Through the glass he saw Frank feint with his left and then level off and send Rocky reeling back from a bone-crushing smash on the jaw.

The thud of it wrung an unconscious grunt of pain out of Ollie, as though he had been the one struck.

Rocky caught a chair and kept himself from going down. Frank was after him. Rocky whipped up the chair and used it as a weapon to fend off further trouble until his head cleared. He was battered and bleeding, his left eye so badly puffed that it was of little use to him. He had given as good as he had received. Whenever he could get in close enough to block those long, punishing rights, he had Frank at his mercy, peppering him with short, pistonlike blows that had the kick of a mule behind them, though they traveled only a few inches.

Rocky's back was to the window. When Grimwood tried to snatch the chair away from him, he swung it over his head so viciously that it slipped out of his hands and went flying through the air. With a shivering crash, it smashed the window, scattering the startled crowd.

Boulder City began to wake up. Many of the merchants on Bridger Street had their living quarters above their establishments. Windows began to go up and heads pop out. Pete Hoffman, homeward bound from an unprofitable poker game, had heard the crashing of glass and ran up the street, seeking an explanation.

"What they fighting about?" he yelled at the constable.

Ollie shook his head. "I dunno, Pete." Uncertainty was creeping up on him. "I don't like to be officious, but they ain't leavin' me no choice, bustin' windows and the like at this time o' night!"

"The way they're going at it, they'll kill each other if they ain't stopped!" Pete jerked out. "If you don't get in there, I will!"

His concern was as much for his hundred shares of Blue Rock Oil as for Rocky and Frank.

A few moments later, with the constable still debating what action he should take, Grimwood was forced back toward the door. Rocky, trying to make the most of his momentary advantage and get in close, leaped at him. They clinched and went down together, striking the door with impact enough to pop it open and spill them out on the sidewalk. They fought there, and across the sidewalk into the street.

Ollie's attempt to get them apart failed miserably. Someone had got word to Ty Roberts. Ollie was glad to see the sheriff elbowing his way through the onlookers.

Ty ordered Pete and the constable to get hold of Rocky. He took care of Frank himself.

"I don't know what this is all about," he growled, "but it's gone far enough! The two of you git inside. The rest of you boys break it up and git along about your business."

Herding the two struggling men into the office, with Pete's help, he sat them down. Posting the constable outside to see that the crowd dispersed and a fresh one didn't gather, he pulled down the window shades and turned to Rocky and Frank.

"Yo're a fine lookin' sight, the two of you!" he stormed indignantly. "What's got into you? I'm mad enough to lock up both of you. The whole town dependin' on you to pull together, and you come up with this sort of thing! What's the idea?"

Rocky shook his head sullenly.

"Better forget it, Ty," he growled. He glared at Grimwood. "I got nothing to say. Maybe you'll have better luck with him."

Frank's puffed lips lifted contemptuously. "Call it personal and let it go at that," he muttered.

Belatedly, both were thinking of Tony. Boulder City would be buzzing about their quarrel in a few hours. Neither wanted her name brought into it.

"All right!" Ty snapped. "I reckon if you boys want

to make damn fools of yoreselves at this stage of the game, that's your privilege." He turned to Hoffman. "Pete, you walk Rocky to the hotel and put him to bed. His face needs fixin' up. I'll get Frank home."

The news spread like a prairie fire. By breakfast time, tongues were wagging all over town. Charlie Oatman was one of the first to hear. He left home early and stopped at the sheriff's office on his way to the bank, hoping to get some information from Roberts.

"I'm as much in the dark as you are," Ty was compelled to tell him. "They were beatin' each other's brains out when I got there. I got 'em apart and into the office. They wouldn't say a word. Later, I took Frank home and fixed him up best I could. All I could git out of him was that Rocky and him had come to the partin' of the ways. What's this goin' to do to the oil company, Charlie?"

Oatman weighed his answer carefully. "I don't think it will have any great importance. Certainly it won't stop us from striking oil—if the oil is there. If one, or both, tenders his resignation, new men can be elected who'll carry on."

"They won't resign," Ty declared with great positiveness. "You couldn't make me believe that after what I saw last night. Frank will try to force Rocky out, and vice versa."

"That may be the case," Oatman admitted.

He hoped it would, for if such a contest developed, Frank would have the advantage. Continuing on to the bank, Charlie checked off on his fingers the names of a dozen men among the bigger investors who would give Grimwood authority to vote their stock. His own hands might be tied, but the men he had in mind would be enough.

It was a morning devoted to endless speculation regarding the cause of the quarrel. None of the countless ideas that were advanced satisfied Oatman. No one was as anxious to get at the truth as he. When the morning passed without Rocky or Frank putting in an appearance at their offices or the company headquarters, he decided to find the latter and have it out with him. He felt he had to know what had happened or lose his mind.

As he was about to leave the bank, Louie Abramson hurried in and plopped down in a chair at his desk with a weary sigh of relief.

"Sit down, Charlie," he said, mopping his face. "What a morning! I been running back and forth, seeing first one, then the other, and getting nowheres. It was like banging my head against a stone wall. But I finally wore 'em down."

"I don't know whether I follow you, Louie," said Oatman.

"I got Rocky and Frank to bury the hatchet. No love lost between them, I can tell you, but they've agreed to go on working together until the well is shot. It's no secret to you that the company's out of money. Rocky is putting up another three thousand and I'm kicking in with a thousand more. If they watch the nickels, that'll be enough to see us through. Make out a deposit slip. I got the money in my pocket. I'll count it out for you."

Charlie sat there without moving, unable to believe

173

his ears. "I can't understand it, Louie. Do you mean to tell me that after what happened last night they're going to shake hands and go on pulling together?"

"Hardly," said Louie. "As near as I can figure, they hate each other's guts. I don't know why, and after what I've been through this morning, I'm damned if I care. I got something more on my mind than their troubles. If I lose every cent I put into this oil deal, I can stand it, and so can you and old Joe and some others, but there's fellas in this town who put up a hundred or two because they knew we were in that can't afford it. I ain't going to see them let down. It'll be tough enough if the well is a bust. At least they won't be able to say there was any funny business about it."

"And Jeanette listened to that argument?" Oatman was even more incredulous.

"He listened. Frank wanted to throw in the sponge. Rocky is the one we got to depend on now. I'll have the office cleaned up and new glass put in this afternoon. Rocky will be there tomorrow morning, tending to business. Frank's heading for camp tonight. I wish to God he had a little more of Rocky's push and drive. This ain't no time to get discouraged."

It left Oatman as deeply puzzled as ever, and disappointed, too, for he had not doubted that this was the definite, irreparable break between Frank and Rocky that he wanted.

That afternoon, enlightenment came to him from an unexpected source. Rita Warren drove into town and came to the bank at once. She knew Rocky was back and that he and Frank had fought. What they had quarreled about was no mystery to her. She did not want ever to see Rocky again. But she did want to hurt him. To have seen him drawn and quartered would not have been too much.

Oatman got up to greet her. Being wholly unaware of the changed relations between Rocky and her, he made a mental note not to make any reference to what had occurred in the early hours of the morning at the office of the Blue Rock Oil Company.

He need not have bothered, for Rita didn't propose to ignore it.

"I understand Mr. Jeanette is back from San Francisco," she observed guilelessly, as she took the chair Charlie offered.

"He's back," he replied, not comprehending the full significance of her remark at once. "I didn't know he'd been in San Francisco."

"Oh, didn't Tony write you?"

That did it. Oatman's face was gray as he sat down.

16

To learn that Grimwood and Jeanette had
fought over Tony was a staggering blow. Charlie
tried to dissemble his agitation and only partly suc-
ceeded. He pretented to listen to Rita, but his mind
was locked in a vise, his one cogent thought being that
his tangled dealing with Rocky had now reached a
crisis. In the past, he had knuckled under to the man
to protect himself and his position in Boulder City.
Nothing so selfish gripped him now; he had to protect
Tony and not only preserve her good name but make it
impossible for Rocky to make a mess of her life. That
was the important consideration; the rest no longer
mattered. His preoccupation was such that Rita had
to repeat her startling statement, that the Spanish
Ranch was to be put up for sale, before it registered
on him.

"You—you can't mean that, Mrs. Warren," he said,
smothering a little gasp of astonishment.

"But I do," Rita insisted. "I know I'll never get out

of the property anything like what's been spent on it. But my mind is made up. I told Mr. Fitz this noon that we'd be moving to California before snow flies. I'll go down in a day or two and start looking for a place."

Oatman shook his head regretfully; the Warren stable and the Spanish Ranch had been solid landmarks in the life of Boulder City.

"This is a sudden decision, Mrs. Warren?"

"Very sudden," Rita admitted. "I want the bank to handle the sale. If you'll come out, we'll go over everything and set a figure."

Oatman had no heart for business. He proved it by saying, "It's a big place, Mrs. Warren. Buyers don't come along every day. So much of the value is in the buildings, rather than the land, that it isn't likely to appeal to a stockman. Perhaps Mr. Jeanette could do more with it than I. He hasn't been devoting much time to his real estate business of late but—"

"Mr. Jeanette can't do anything for me," Rita informed him, with chilling emphasis. "I prefer doing business with a man I can trust. I'm sure you'll do everything possible, Mr. Oatman."

Though he gave her an opportunity to say what had turned her against Rocky, she did not avail herself of it.

"Found him out," Charlie thought. "Pray God, Tony does."

He told Rita he would get out to the ranch as soon as he could. He was only getting rid of her; his thoughts didn't run as far ahead as a trip to the Spanish Ranch. After she left, he was surprised to find that he had nothing to debate with himself; his course was plainly marked, and he was ready to embark on it. Knowing he would find Rocky in his quarters at the hotel, he left the bank and went down the street at once. At the Boulder Inn, he sent his name up and after a short delay, he was shown upstairs.

"I can imagine why you're here," Rocky told him, refusing to be embarrassed by the condition of his face.

"I'll leave you in no doubt about it," Charlie replied, after making sure the door was closed. "You knocked the bottom out of your game, Jeanette, when you ran down to California to see my daughter. I don't know what took place between you, and I prefer not to know. I'm not going to waste any words about this; I'm giving you twenty-four hours to settle up your affairs. If you're still in town after the 3:15 pulls out tomorrow, I'm going up to the courthouse and make a full statement to the District Attorney."

Rocky met it with a sneer.

"You're bluffing, Oatman. Smearing Tony with your own mistake is the last thing in the world you'll do. You can't open your mouth without shaming her."

"I've thought of that, Jeanette," Charlie flashed back. "If I knew any other way to show you up, I'd take it. But this is the only way. I hope you'll stay and face it. I'll never know for certain that Tony's safe from you until you've been shown up for what you really are. It'll more than repay her for any shame that comes to her because of my wrongdoing."

Rocky thought this was only the beginning, but Oatman had nothing further to say. Opening the door, he stepped out and descended the stairs. The gray look that had been touching his face with increasing frequency of late, came again as he crossed the lobby. Suddenly, his hand flew to his heart and he had to find a chair until the knifelike pain passed. He had been to see Wingaard recently. The doctor had warned him to avoid all excitement.

Avoid excitement! Charlie thought of it after the seizure passed. What fools these doctors were! They examined a man's body. They knew nothing of what a man's life was. They could tell you to avoid excitement, but they didn't tell you how to avoid it.

Rocky had no intention of leaving town. He was at the office in the morning, looking more presentable. Judge Bonfils nodded curtly as he passed but did not stop for a minute or two, as he usually did. Rocky understood why. Other old friends nodded, too, but hurried on. It made him realize that he was no longer the popular hero. A list of meats and groceries for the camp had to be made out. He had it ready when Louie came in. The latter took exception to some of the items.

"I don't know what they do with all the coffee we send out," he complained. "They must feed it to the mules. Cut it down to ten pounds, Rocky, and they'll have to go easy on it. And why maple syrup? Let 'em use corn syrup."

He crossed off an item or two.

"Good food and plenty of it is all right, but we ain't putting up no more banquets for that crew."

Rocky smiled. If he had a friend left in town it was Louie Abramson.

"You going to the club this noon?" Louie asked.

"Why not?" Rocky returned. "Everyone in town knows I'm sporting a black eye."

The luncheon was as boistrous as ever. The Judge was the current chairman. He had a fellow jurist from Laramie as a guest. Rocky found his chief interest in the fact that Charlie Oatman was not present. On inquiring the reason, he learned that Doc Wingaard had been called to the Oatman home that morning.

"Nothing serious," Bill Brown, the druggist, told Rocky. "But Charlie's got a bad heart; he ought to take things easy."

Rocky left early and went back to the office. When it got to be half-past two, he started watching the clock. With Oatman sick, he found more reason than ever to believe that nothing would come of the threat to expose him. And yet, as the deadline neared, he refused to sit there, waiting. Locking up, he walked up the street to the sheriff's office. From there he could see whoever climbed the long flight of stone steps to the courthouse.

Ty was not unfriendly, though he had less to say than usual. Rocky stuck it out, doing his best to kill time. He heard the afternoon train for the West pull out. There was no sign of Oatman.

"Just a bluff," Rocky told himself. "I was a sucker to give it a second thought."

After another few minutes, he got up to leave, only to freeze in his tracks. Charlie Oatman was climbing the courthouse steps, and obviously with a great effort.

"Well, I'll be damned!" Rocky muttered to himself. "He's going through with it!"

"What'd you say?" Ty asked.

"Nothing!" Rocky growled. "When you want me, I'll be at the office."

His first impulse was to grab a horse and flee town.

"It wouldn't do me any good to run now; it's too late," he decided. "I wouldn't get far; I'm too well known."

The house of cards he had built lay in complete ruin. He had to have someone to blame.

"Rita, damn her!" he raged. "If she'd only kept her mouth shut!"

He wished he had back the three thousand he had handed over to Louie the previous morning; money would get him a good lawyer. Maybe he could beat this rap; the only evidence against him was the series of admissions he had made to Oatman. If found guilty, he'd be a first offender. That would work in his favor. He didn't fear that standing trial for the First National job would be followed by indictments in other Wyoming towns.

"They couldn't make anything stick—unless they slap some fingerprints at me," he told himself. "I'll make bail and give them a fight. Even if I'm sent over the road, it won't be for more than five years and I can cut that to three with good behavior."

But it was all so needless. That was what floored him. He could have had everything he wanted if he hadn't lost his head over Tony. He had no blame for her; she was clean and decent and he'd never find another like her. But no woman was worth what she was costing him.

He let himself into the office. Before leaving, he had drawn the shades. He didn't raise them now; he wanted to wait there alone.

The detachment that had once been his best defense was no longer his; the few months he had lived in Boulder City had changed him more than he realized.

A map of Mustard Valley was pasted on the wall. A bitter, croaking laugh welled out of him as his harried eyes fell on it.

"Wouldn't it be a laugh if what I started put this burg on the map, after all, and made millionaires of some of these yokels!"

He had not been sitting there long when he heard someone run past. Others ran by. A man called across the street to another. Rocky couldn't make out what he said, but he caught Oatman's name.

"I guess that settles it!" he growled. "He's made his squawk!"

Fifteen minutes passed, with unmistakable excitement running up and down Bridger Street. A shadow fell across the door and Ty Roberts stood there.

"Charlie Oatman," he began, as he stepped in, "he's dead. Collapsed in the D.A.'s office."

"Well—?" Rocky demanded, wanting him to continue.

Not knowing what was on Rocky's mind, Ty said, "It was all over in a few moments."

"What about the statement he went up there to make?" Rocky demanded.

"Statement? He made no statement. He keeled over just as he came through the door. Where'd you git the idea he had any statement to make to Murtagh?"

"Why, I figured he must have had something on his mind, to get out of a sick bed and go up to the courthouse."

"I hadn't thought of that," Ty muttered, satisfied with Rocky's explanation. "Losin' Charlie Oatman is goin' to be a blow to this town . . . Can I depend on you to git word to Frank Grimwood?"

"I'll send somebody out right away," Rocky assured him. "If there's anything else I can do, let me know."

He slumped down in his chair after Ty left, tension draining out of him and leaving him weak. What a break! All his anxiety and torment had been for nothing.

Frank arrived in town early the next morning. After making himself presentable, he went on to the Oatmans'. Tony was hurrying back from the Coast but would not be in Boulder City for another forty-eight hours. Around town, business was largely at a standstill, with the oil venture temporarily forgotten. In death, Charles Albert Oatman was receiving a tribute from his fellow citizens such as he had never enjoyed in life.

It was noon before Grimwood walked in on Rocky. Both were coldly hostile. Rocky asked about the well.

"We're drilling night and day," said Frank. "But we're running out of casing. We'll have to shoot in another week to ten days." His eyes narrowed as he faced Rocky. "Charlie Oatman died knowing why we went to it."

It hardly came under the heading of news to Rocky.

"He didn't get anything out of me," he flung back belligerently.

"I know that. He got it from Rita. She came in to see him the next day about selling the ranch. She let something slip."

"Slip, eh?" Rocky jeered. "Any old day! That dame knew what she was doing."

"And so did you," Frank flung back accusingly. "Between the two of you, you put Charlie in his grave."

Rocky leaped to his feet, ready to start swinging again; but the charge was so true that even his stony conscience was not proof against it.

"Have it your way, if it'll make you feel any better," he growled.

Grimwood gave him a withering glance. "No question about how I feel," he said, on his way out.

Rocky's savage mood passed and he fell to a realistic examination of the future. He was on his own now; he had lost his ace-in-the-hole, but there was compensation in the fact that his past was now dead and buried as deeply as Oatman would be in a day or two. It led him to ask himself why he shouldn't step into Oatman's shoes.

It opened an interesting vista of thought that appealed to his ego. If the company struck oil, he'd be riding high again. Play his cards right and he could take over this town and make himself a more important man than Oatman ever had been.

After Tony got back, he saw nothing of her until he went to the church for the funeral services. She sat with her mother and Frank and several relatives from Rawlins and Casper. He found her more beautiful and precious than ever in her sorrow. Whenever he tore his eyes away from her, it was only for a moment.

Rita was among those present, and as attractive as ever. Rocky had only a vast contempt for her. Quite by accident, they came face to face, after the services were over and the funeral procession was forming for the short drive to the cemetery.

Rita looked a hole through him and was about to continue on to her carriage. The moment was too much for her, however, and she couldn't forego this opportunity to let him feel her venom.

"I'm surprised that you had the effrontery to show your face here," she said, for his ears alone.

"I was thinking the same about you," Rocky retorted. "Grimwood says the two of us put Oatman in his grave. Maybe he knows what he's talking about."

In Boulder City, as elsewhere, the threads that had been broken by the passing of a prominent citizen, had to be picked up and a new fabric begun.

A week passed before Tony ventured down-town. Rocky made no attempt to see her; and then one noon, several days later, he found her lunching alone at the Boulder Inn. On his way out, he stopped at her table.

Tony raised her eyes, silently imploring him to leave.

"Please——" she murmured, as he lingered on. "We haven't anything to say to one another, Rocky."

"Is everything all right with you and Frank?" he asked.

"Yes—of course. Mother will announce the engagement at an appropriate time."

"That's all I wanted to know," he told her. "I scrambled things for myself. I'm glad I didn't mix up everything for you."

17

THE STEER SHIPPING WAS ON. BEEF HERDS FROM JOE
Creek, Seven Springs and other districts were arriving
daily in Boulder City. They were coming so fast now
that they could not be accommodated in the railroad cor-
rals, and it was not an uncommon sight to see two or
three of the big outfits holding their cattle on the bed
grounds south of town, while they awaited their turn.

Cattle money had always been the blood and sinew
and backbone of the town's prosperity. Boulder City,
or at least that considerable segment of its citizens who
had purchased stock in the Blue Rock Oil Company,
had never been more keenly aware of it than now. The
cattle business was a solid business. You could turn
young calves out on the range, see them grow to ma-
turity, drive them into town and ship them off to
Omaha or Chicago and be reasonably sure of what the
returns would be. It was different with oil; no one
could tell what a drill was likely to find, down in the
bowels of the earth.

Out in Mustard Valley, the well was sinking deeper and deeper, and Boulder City's confidence in the outcome was sinking with it. As the season had advanced, the prevailing northwesterly winds had begun to blow with a foretaste of their winter vigor, making the drive to the valley anything but a pleasant experience. But it was the pessimism that had set in, rather than the physical discomfort involved, that had reduced the Sunday stream of visitors to a trickle.

The drillers were now down over twenty-eight hundred feet. Only a few lengths of casing remained. Knowing the well would, of necessity, have to be shot before the week was out, Rocky locked up the office in town and established himself at the camp.

With the issue so soon to be decided, and the hope that the well would bring itself in almost extinguished, Grimwood was in a surly mood, his nerves on edge. Even if relations between him and Rocky had been friendly, he would have been difficult to get along with. Since the reverse was true, they were snapping at each other continually.

On the way out, Rocky had not failed to notice the activity at the Spanish Ranch. Freighting wagons, piled high with boxes and crates of furnishings, were being loaded in the yard. Rita and her personal servants had already left for California. After shipping the horses, Mr. Fitz had taken charge of the tremendous job of closing up the place.

Rocky had tried to tell himself it didn't matter. But it did; the Spanish Ranch had figured very prominently in some of his shattered dreams. They would have come true if he had been content to let well enough alone. Therein lay the real bitterness of the situation for him. His fortunes wouldn't have been hanging on the dubious returns from a hole in the ground; he would have had money, position, the seductive charms of Rita Warren to keep him amused. He had kicked it all away. If he snarled at Frank it was because he knew he had not only kicked everything away, but had got nothing in return.

From the open doorway of the headquarters cabin, he saw Grimwood and Getty step off the floor of the rig and engage in a heated argument. They turned his way then, continuing their discussion as they came to the door.

"What's the argument?" Rocky inquired.

"No argument," Getty answered. "Grimwood says it's now or never; that there's no sense going on working till we haven't a piece of casing left. We've got very little left, it's true. Tomorrow, or the day after, we'll have to call a halt. I say, go on till we're forced to stop. It could make a difference."

"A few feet more won't make any difference," Frank countered. "If the oil is there, we'll get it."

"I'll take Getty's word for that," said Rocky. "John, this ain't the first well you've put down. You're the expert we've been depending on. When will you hit twenty-nine hundred feet?"

"About noon tomorrow."

Rocky's eyes focused on Grimwood. "Is there any reason why we can't go that far?" His belligerent tone indicated how little was required to unseat the chip he carried on his shoulder.

"I don't suppose there is," Frank muttered with equal hostility.

"Okay!" Getty agreed. "When we hit twenty-nine hundred, we bring the tools up for the last time and begin to clear away and get ready to shoot. In the meantime, you better get some men and teams busy with the scrapers and finish the sump. If we get oil in any quantity, you're going to need it. No telling how quick a well can be capped."

The sump consisted of an earthen embankment across the lower end of the valley. That afternoon Grimwood and Rocky got out with the men and had it completed by nightfall.

The drilling stopped temporarily, shortly after eight the following morning. Getty came to the door of the shack to speak to Frank and Rocky. "We'll be hitting twenty-nine hundred by eleven o'clock. It'll take us another three hours to remove the tools, clear the rig floor and get up the nitro. By the middle of the afternoon, we'll be all set to drop the iron. You talked of having some folks come out from town to see us touch her off. There's time for 'em to get here if you send word in now."

He went back to the platform and after a few minutes, the drill began biting again.

"Louie would like to be here," said Rocky. "We gave him our word we wouldn't forget to send for him."

Frank nodded woodenly. "I'd like to have Tony present. I don't believe she'd come."

"Because of me?" Rocky's face had whipped flat. "That needn't bother either one of you; I'll keep out of the way. There's nothing for you to do here. If you're going into town, you better be on your way. Getty said three o'clock."

Grimwood had been gone several hours, when the blowing of the steam whistle on the boiler brought Rocky to the door. Getty's roughnecks (in his oil field parlance, he never referred to his men by any other term) raised a yell. They had reached the end of the drilling. The tools were brought up and the bailer put down for the final time.

Rocky ate dinner with Getty and the crew. The men were nervous and restrained.

"They're acting like a lot of prima donnas on the opening night of a show," Rocky remarked to big John.

"They've shot a lot of wells in their time, but they'll never get over being hepped up when it comes to the last few hours. They haven't got a dollar invested in the hole, but they're just as excited as you are."

After dinner, the tools were removed and the platform cleared and made ready for the lowering of the cans of nitro. The explosive had been stored in a tent, half a mile from the scene of operations.

It was after two o'clock, when Getty spoke to one of his roughnecks, telling him he could drive out to the tent and start loading. "Take Martin with you, and be a little more careful than usual when you put the stuff in the wagon. It's been out there under the sun a few days. That never improves its disposition. No need to hurry; the folks coming out from town ain't in sight yet."

It was only a few minutes later, however, when Rocky saw a line of buggies and other vehicles moving over road. They arrived before the nitro wagon came up from the tent. With Grimwood came Tony, Louie Abramson and Doc Wingaard. Louie was keyed up to a pitch of excitement that left his face ashen. Rocky spoke to Tony, but it was only an impersonal word or two. His glance followed her as Grimwood led her around the well to the headquarters shack. Though striking oil would mean riches, perhaps great wealth, for him, he told himself it would be an empty success without having her to share it.

The crowd of a score or more that had come out from Boulder City immediately got in Getty's way. He ordered them back. They obliged, but every few minutes he had to speak to them again. When he saw the nitro wagon coming, he halted the work and really spoke his mind. "I been patient with you folks. Now you're going to step back and keep back, or this well won't be shot this afternoon. It's dangerous up here. There's enough nitroglycerin in that wagon to blow everyone of you to bits if it goes off."

Rocky and Wingaard stood together, to the left of the well. Grimwood and Tony looked on from the doorway of the shack. Doc called Rocky's attention to them.

"They're almost on top of the well," he said, with some anxiety. "It doesn't look safe to me, but I guess Frank knows what he's doing; he's had some experience with oil wells."

"They'll be all right there," said Rocky. "They've got a roof over their heads; they won't be conked with a piece of falling rock. If fire breaks out, they can slip through the back door."

Getty waved to the two men on the nitro wagon and they drove up to the platform. Dan Christopher, the boss driller, had been attracted to the well-head by a faint hissing. He put his ear down to the open blowout preventer, attached to the tip of the casing. What he heard made him spring to his feet. "John, come here quick!" he cried.

Getty hurried to the hole and listened. He knew instantly what that gulping and hissing as of a thousand snakes meant.

"Gas!" he yelled. "Close the blowout valve!" Running to the edge of the platform, he shouted instructions at the two men on the wagon, ordering them to drive away at once. Not depending on anyone else to do it, he dashed to the boiler and pulled the fire. With Rocky's assistance, he doused the coals, making sure they were thoroughly out.

"How bad is this likely to be?" Rocky asked.

Grimwood ran up in time to catch Getty's answer.

"There's no telling how bad it may be!" big John growled. "If gas is all we've got there may be enough of it to blow everything sky high! No need for you fellas to stand here! Get inside the shack, or drop back there with the others!"

"John, the well may be coming in by itself," Frank exclaimed, catching the contractor by the arm. "They'll do it this way sometimes."

"I know it! I hope that's the case! But if she's an out and out gasser, we may have trouble!"

He ran around to the other side of the platform, barking instructions to his men. Frank stood there as one transfixed, his face drawn and colorless. He had waited a long time for this moment.

"Snap out of it!" Rocky growled. "Get back inside with Tony! If the well catches fire, you get her out the back way in a hurry!"

To his surprise, Frank turned away without a retort.

They had barely parted, when they felt the earth tremble. From somewhere down in the depths came a low growling.

Rocky saw one of the roustabouts point to the casing head. It was shaking violently. Getty began screaming at his men to run for it. He dashed past Rocky and Wingaard, shouting, "Get down! She's going to go!" He ran on a few feet and threw himself to the ground.

Frank had darted into the headquarters shack, pulling Tony away from the door. He was just in time. With a sharp thunderlike clap, the blowout preventer was torn loose from the casing and went hurtling through the crown of the derrick. Instantly the air was filled with a deafening piano scream as the released gas shot upward, rising a hundred feet above the derrick and enveloping it momentarily in a diaphanous vapor. An explosion followed that was heard as far away as the Spanish Ranch. The crown block and its pulleys went skyward.

The debris that went up had to come down. A heavy pulley fell where Rocky and Grimwood had been standing but a moment before and ploughed into the ground.

Getty got to his knees, thinking the worst was over. A stream of gas, gravel and salt water was shooting into the air and rising high above the rig. Fire was the great danger now. All that was needed to ignite the gas was for a fragment of rock to strike the steel casing in a way to cause a spark.

Frank was as grimly aware of that threat as Getty. "We better run out the back way," he told Tony. "I've seen gas fires. It's like a flash of lightning. A spark will do it. The place would be ablaze from end to end before we could move."

He spoke too late. Before they could take a step, a second explosion that made the first sound like the harmless snapping of a firecracker knocked them flat and brought the shack crashing down around them.

The terrific blast leveled every building in camp. Of the rig, only the tottering derrick remained. Bullwheel, walking beam, sampson post, the whole draw works, were gone. A hundred yards away, the boiler was rolling and bouncing through the brush.

John Getty got to his feet, dazed but unhurt. His men had come through unscathed. Down at the barn, injured horses were screaming and the freighting crew was trying to lead them out of the wreckage.

Getty, starting to run to the shattered cabin, glanced at the well and what he saw stopped him in his tracks. Bug-eyed, he watched the earth's crust rise in a great blister that stood up like the hunched back of an angry cat. He knew what it meant. The amount of gas trying to reach the surface was so great that the casing couldn't accommodate it and it was welling up around the casing and shooting up through the earth. The top of the blister was blown off a moment later. The gas whistled briefly as it escaped. The ground began to settle back, then. It set the tottering derrick to weaving back and forth so violently that it threatened to come down any moment.

Dan Christopher, the boss driller, ran up. "Come on, John!" he cried. "Grimwood and the girl are trapped in there! If we don't get them out in a hurry, we won't get them out at all!"

"Look!" Big John gasped, pointing to the well.

A black, glistening fountain was spouting from the casing head, rising higher and higher.

"It's oil!" Christopher cried. "It's oil, Rocky!" he repeated as the latter dashed up to them.

"Oil, and to hell with it!" Rocky snarled. "Look at that derrick! It's going to fall across the shack! They'll be killed! Get a move on you!"

They reached the shack and wrested aside a section of the shattered roof.

"You alive in there?" Rocky called, gritting his teeth against the possible answer.

"We're all right," Tony returned, her voice uneven and off key. "I barely got a scratch. Frank's pinned to the floor but he says it's nothing serious."

Relief flooded through Rocky leaving him weak for a moment. "Thank God, you're all right!" he got out hoarsely. "Don't move, Tony, or some more of this junk may come down on you. Just stay where you are; we'll get you out."

Worming his way through the wreckage of 2 x 4's and pine siding, he passed back to Getty and Christopher pieces of splintered scantling and a door frame that came free without disturbing the whole mass. Ignoring the sharp ends of the twisted nails that scratched his hands and arms, he reached her. There wasn't room for him to lift her or even turn her around. But by putting his arms under her shoulders, he managed to drag her out, head first. Her face was smudged and her hair disheveled, but he had never found her so utterly desirable.

"We'll go after Frank," he said, handing her over to Doc Wingaard.

He reached Grimwood without difficulty, only to tug at him in vain. "Can't move you an inch," he rapped. "Your legs feel broken?"

"No, they're numb, but they don't feel broken," Frank told him.

"This whole corner of the roof is pinning you down." Rocky raised his voice to Getty and the driller, telling them to find a 2 x 4 and use it as a pry. "If you can lift this junk an inch or two, I can drag him out."

The two men stepped back to find something that would serve. As they did, a shadow moved quickly across the sky. Christopher looked up, and a terror-laden scream was wrenched from his lips. Rocky and Big John flicked a quick glance skyward, too. Appalled by what they saw, they froze in their tracks. Not that running would have helped them now; Christopher's warning had come too late and the anguished cry of the crowd was only a useless overtone. The swaying pendulum of heavy timbers and three-inch planking had been swinging back and forth in an ever widening arc. As Rocky and the others watched, spellbound, the heavy derrick stood perfectly still for a split second as it hovered precariously over their heads. The next moment it came hurtling down, breaking up like match-sticks as it fell.

Though only the upper section struck the already shattered cabin, it completely flattened what was left of the flimsy building, burying Rocky and the others in the ruins.

Several members of Getty's crew, together with the teamsters and swampers, all of whom had escaped serious injury when the barn collapsed, rushed up to begin the work of rescuing the trapped men. Louie Abramson, Doc Wingaard and a dozen more of the visitors assisted as best they could. A fountain of oil was spouting from the well, but that was a secondary consideration just now.

The wind began to whip away the clouds of dust that hovered over the scene of the disaster. From where she watched, a few yards away, Tony saw John Getty and his driller brought out. The two men were badly shaken but, miraculously, they had suffered only superficial cuts and bruises. It was a different story with Rocky. Doc Wingaard climbed over the wreckage to him and immediately ordered him placed on a blanket.

"Doctor Wingaard!" Tony cried as she ran up. "Is he—is he badly hurt?"

"I can't say for the present," Doc told her. "A timber hit him and laid his scalp open. He's unconscious. If it's just the scalp wound, there's nothing to worry about; a few stitches will take care of that." He turned to the men carrying Rocky. "Take him down toward the barn and place him in the shade of one of those overturned wagons. I'll be along in a moment."

He took Tony's arm and walked aside with her.

"You've got to keep your chin up, honey," he said in his kindly way. "I've got bad news for you."

"Frank?" she gasped.

Doc nodded. "I just had a look at him. A piece of heavy timber struck him. There were spikes in it ... He couldn't have suffered. I'm sure it was all over in a moment."

He put his arm around her as he saw her sway.

"I'm awfully sorry, Tony. I liked Frank Grimwood, and I know what he meant to you."

His arm tightened as he felt a sob shake her. Being wiser than most men, he didn't attempt to restrain her. When she was able to speak, she said:

"I can't believe he's gone—not this way ... To have his dream realized, and pay such a price for it!" She raised her eyes, and they were wells of unhappiness. "They quarreled over me—Frank and Rocky. Everyone knows it. It was all my fault. I—I can't help feeling guilty."

"There's no reason why you should." Doc's voice was fatherly, yet stern. "It would be wonderful if we could arrange our lives as we pleased. But that never happens; we're tossed about like tumbleweeds." He was thinking as much of his daughter Bonnie as of Tony. "These things happen, and we feel we can't go on. But we do. It's remarkable how life corrects most of its mistakes, give it time ... I'll have to get Rocky to town as quickly as I can. I'd like to have you drive in with me. I'll ask Louie Abramson to go, too. There're three or four women in the crowd. They'd be glad to comfort you. Shall I call them over, Tony?"

"No," she murmured, "I prefer to be alone for a few minutes ... I'll be all right, Doctor."

When consciousness returned to Rocky, he found Tony and Wingaard kneeling at his side, with Getty and Louie and half a dozen others peering down at him anxiously.

"Rocky! Are you going to be all right?" Tony cried.

He grinned and said, "Sure! I guess I been out cold for some time. Something hit me on the head."

"Just take it easy," Wingaard advised. "Something hit you on the head, sure enough. I've washed your face and done what I could, but I've got to get you to the hospital and make some permanent repairs . . . How do you feel?

"Shaky," Rocky admitted. "When I saw that derrick plunging down, I figured it was curtains for the four of us." His glance traveled around the ring of faces. "I see you, John, and Dan—where's Grimwood?"

He read his answer in the quick tightening of their faces. It was Louie who spoke. "Frank didn't make it, Rocky."

Full comprehension of what had happened came slowly to Rocky. Suddenly, he tried to sit up. Wingaard forced him down, saying, "None of that! I don't want that scalp wound to start bleeding again. For the last time, I'm telling you to take it easy."

Frank killed! Somehow, it was incredible. Many times of late Rocky had speculated on what was to be the ultimate end of their relations. It had never occurred to him that it was to be this. He gazed at Tony. She was crying softly. He murmured her name, but her eyes failed to meet his. Figuratively, it was equivalent to plunging a knife into his heart. Frank was gone, he told himself, but she was now more un-attainable than ever.

With the callousness he often affected to hide his true feelings, he looked at Getty and said, "We hit oil, eh?"

"Plenty of it," big John told him. "The sump's filling up. Before sundown, we'll have the well capped. Mustard Valley's going to make a field, all right."

"Great!" Rocky muttered, with a grin. "It'll put Boulder City on the map. That's what I wanted. No-body can take that away from me."

18

LITTLE LOUIE ABRAMSON, GETTING RICHER BY THE minute, hurried into the offices of the Blue Rock Oil Company and sat down with Rocky. "I've changed my plans about the addition to the store," he declared, exuding enthusiasm. "I'm going to make it five stories instead of three. The business will be here in a year to support it."

"Sounds all right to me," Rocky said. "Boulder City is busting out at the seams already. Wait till spring comes; you won't know the town. I hear you bought all that land along Squaw Creek. What are you going to do with it?"

"I'm going to cut it up into lots and put up some houses. It's mighty pretty along the creek. It'll make a fine addition. I ain't going to call it Abramson's addition, neither; I'm going to give it a fancy name. You know what?"

"No—"

"Jeanette Park." Louie beamed at him proudly.

"Why put my name on it?" Rocky demanded, scowling.

"Why? We owe everything to you. Frank had an idea but he wouldn't have got anywhere without you. He was ready to quit, wasn't he? It's going to be called Jeanette Park." Louie grinned mischievously. "I ain't stopping there; I bought the old Spanish Ranch this morning."

Rocky sat up, amazed. "You're crazy, Louie! I always thought you had your feet on the ground. It's no good as a cow ranch. Don't tell me you're going in for fast horses."

"No, sir! I ain't going to run it as a ranch; I'm going to turn it into a hotel. It's the nearest place to Mustard Valley. Men are flocking in. They can't live out there in tents through a Wyoming winter—at least, they won't if I can put a roof over their heads. The Wyoming & Western is going right ahead with its freight spur to the field. Don't you be surprised if they build a depot in my front yard, come April or May."

Rocky shook his head. "You always seem to do all right, Louie."

"Not always, Rocky; I'm a sucker when it comes to pinochle."

The first snow lay on the ground already. Two months had passed since the pioneer well had come in. No less than eleven wells were being put down, two of them on the property of the Blue Rock Oil Company. Matt Hughes, the barber, had removed the chairs and mirrors from his establishment and turned it into a Stock Exchange, complete with blackboard and a Western Union ticker. Oil stocks and quotations on leases were listed, with changes occurring every hour. If you wanted to find anyone, the saying was to look for him at the Stock Exchange. The mad scramble for land had received a jolt when the U. S. Navy had stepped in and declared the southern fringe of the Blue Rock a Navy oil reserve. The net effect of that order had been to boom the price of what land was left open to entry.

For stockmen, winter brought the usual season of inactivity. Not so for the infant oil industry; the road to Mustard Valley was being kept open and a small army of laborers was proceeding rapidly with the construction of the railroad spur that was to tap the field. No less than four of the big oil companies had moved in and were drilling. There was talk of a refinery for Boulder City; shipping crude half way across the country in tank cars gave the railroads too large a bite of the profits.

Rocky employed a secretary and typist now and had bought some new furniture. Louie was of the opinion that the company should move to more imposing quarters. When Rocky walked to the door with him this morning, he mentioned it again.

"We ought to get out of this place," he argued. "We can afford to put up a modern building of our own that'll do the company credit. If you don't want to go that far, why not see what you can do about leasing the ground floor of the Oatman Building?"

"Louie, you don't find oil in an office," said Rocky. "This little joint has been lucky for us. Leave well enough alone; if anybody wants to do business with us, they can find us."

After they parted, Rocky walked up the street to the

Stock Exchange and looked at the board. He found a crowd there, including Sheriff Roberts. Ty gave him a warm greeting, as did many others. Judge Bonfils was present, and just leaving. He gave Rocky a brief nod that was in keeping with his coolness to him since Rita Warren had left Wyoming so suddenly. Aside from Ira Bonfils, the town was at Rocky's feet. If others were prosperous, he was more so. But riches and acclaim brought no happiness or peace of mind. Tony and her mother had gone east to spend the winter. She had left without a word. He found little satisfaction in telling himself she would be back; that she had only run away from him for a few months.

Blue Rock Oil was up again today. After spending only a few minutes in the Exchange, Rocky walked back up the street, restlessness gnawing at him. To the north, the skies were leaden.

"More snow on the way," he muttered. It gave him a feeling of being locked in. "I might as well face it; she's just letting me down the easy way. She's shown me where I get off. If I had any guts, I'd grab a train and get out of this burg, instead of being cooped up here, waiting for her to come home."

The weeks passed without bringing him any word from her. Just before the Christmas holidays, it snowed for thirty-eight hours. Boulder City dug itself out of the drifts and made merry. Out in the valley, John Getty and the host of men who had come out from Pennsylvania at his urging, cursed the Wyoming winter and threatened to take the next train back east. The railroad spur to the field had been completed. The men commuted back and forth to Louie's Spanish Inn

(he had christened it without consulting anyone),
where he and Rocky played host to them at a boisterous
Christmas Day dinner.

Rocky still lived at the Boulder. He could have gone
out every evening if he had accepted the invitations
that were pressed on him. If he declined, it was only
because they spelled complete boredom. Louie had
taught him how to play pinochle. They got together
several nights a week, business at the Bon Ton permitting. It was his only relaxation. Then, one evening,
late in January, Louie startled him with the announcement that he was leaving for Kansas City the following
day to get married.

Louie was gone two weeks, leaving Rocky to his own
devices. When he returned with his attractive young
bride, there was no resumption of the pinochle games.
Loneliness began to eat into Rocky. It had never bothered him before. He had time on his hands in which to
think things over now—things which he wanted to dis-
miss from his mind forever. He tried, but they were
always there, ready to spring at him unbidden. To get
away from himself, he took to dropping in at Doc Wingaard's office in the evening. He was fond of Doc
and could throw off most of his restraint with him.

It was getting well along into February. A warm
Chinook blew for several days, taking away most of
the snow. But it was only a temporary respite; winter
was not relaxing its grip on Wyoming for another five
or six weeks. Depressed, Rocky began telling himself
again that he was going to leave Boulder City. He
mentioned it one night to Wingaard.

"I'll keep my stock, but I'll step out of the company,"

he said. "I don't know where I'll go. Texas, maybe."

Doc, who understood him much better than he suspected, asked if he had heard from Tony.

"No," Rocky told him. "No reason why she should write to me."

"Strange, but I thought there was," said Wingaard. "She didn't consult me about going east for the winter. If she had, I would have advised her to go. I know it's the best thing she could have done. By the way you've been brooding and distressing yourself, it's easy to see that you think she ran out on you."

"Well, what else is there to think?" Rocky muttered.

"She was engaged to Frank. She had just lost her father. What did you expect her to do—come rushing to you? There's a fitness about things, Rocky, that you don't seem to understand. Even if she did run out on you, are you going to help matters by running out on her? I don't care how far you run, you won't be able to get away from yourself. You didn't ask me for my advice, so you don't have to take it. But if it were me, I'd stick."

Rocky shook his head grimly. "You don't understand, Doc; there's other reasons why I should go. I'm not going to explain what I mean. I may miss the fitness of a lot of things, but not this."

He lay awake half the night, thinking about Tony and himself. Without comprehending what he was doing, he had been exploring his conscience for weeks and moving ever nearer to a decision. He was face to face with it at last. Seeing it so clearly, he didn't try to evade the issue. For five months he had lived outside the law. He had robbed a bank and looted express

207

offices. No one knew, and there was no chance now that anyone ever would know. But *he* knew. Come what would, it must always remain an insurmountable barrier between Tony and him. He wondered why he had never realized it before. Though it was something quite apart from the matter of whether she loved him or not, it would always be there to cost him her love. The only way that barrier could be leveled would be to confess the truth. To do that would cast him out of her life forever.

"It's better for both of us that it ends this way," he growled to himself, after brooding over it for hours. "If she were mine for the asking, I couldn't take her without coming clean. I stacked the deck against myself at the start and it's too late to do anything about it now."

In the days that followed, his determination to leave Boulder City grew. He sold his insurance business, now profitable in spite of his neglect, and disposed of several small pieces of business real estate. By the middle of March, he was ready to disassociate himself from the affairs of the oil company. A meeting of the officers of the corporation was at hand. That would be the time for him to speak. On Thursday, he attended the weekly luncheon of the Business Men's Club. It was the first time in several weeks that he had been present. After the meeting broke up, old Joe Evans and Hank Taylor asked him to walk back to the bank. Old Joe was still chairman of the board that controlled the First National. What they had to tell him was no less than that they wanted to elect him to the board and name him president of the institution.

"We didn't hurry to elect anybody to Charlie's place because we've had the idea for some time that you was the man we wanted," old Joe said.

"That's right," Taylor agreed. "It ain't only what you've done for the town that we're thinkin' of. It's goin' to take a big man to fill Charlie Oatman's shoes. We know you can do it, Rocky."

Rocky was overwhelmed, as much by the irony of what they were offering him as anything else. A few months back, he would have given an arm for this opportunity. This afternoon, the brass and ruthlessness that once had been so characteristic in him fled in confusion before some unsuspected streak of decency, and to his surprise, he heard himself saying no.

"Don't turn us down without thinkin' it over!" old Joe protested. "I know yo're busy, but we can work it out."

"I appreciate your offering it to me," said Rocky, his eyes dark with his thinking. "But I can't take it; I'm leaving town in a couple weeks."

"Leavin'?" the two old cowmen demanded as one.

"Why, we figgered you was a fixture around here!" old Joe exclaimed. "What's happened?"

"Not a thing," Rocky answered stolidly. "I just figure it's time for me to be moving on."

Old Joe carried that news home with him. His daughter, Jinny Belle, had been corresponding with Tony. She got a letter off posthaste. Five days later Tony was back in Boulder City. Spring was in the air again, but it had nothing to do with her excitement. Pausing at the house only long enough to refresh herself and don a new gray whipcord suit that she had purchased in New York, she hurried down-town.

Rocky was alone in the office with his secretary, when he saw her coming. He leaped to his feet and was at the door before her hand touched it. Sight of her changed everything; all his carefully taken resolves and plans suddenly meant nothing.

"I—I hadn't expected you back so soon," he managed to say. "When did you get in?"

"On the late afternoon train. Mother is busy unpacking. Nothing in the house for dinner, of course. She sent me down to order some things sent up." She had herself so well in hand that this bit of polite fabrication went unquestioned in Rocky's mind.

Tony was acquainted with Mollie Downs, his secretary. She spoke to Mollie and remarked how busy Boulder City seemed. From her tone one might have thought that she had been gone only a day or two.

Rocky never took his eyes off her. "Won't you come in and sit down?"

"I better not," Tony said with an apologetic smile. "The market will be closing in a few minutes; I want to catch the last delivery. I thought if you weren't going to be busy this evening you might come up to the studio."

"What time?" he asked, his voice low but warm and eager. How even her teeth were! How perfect her lips! And that strange glow on her young face! A man could well lose the world for her and have the better of the bargain.

"Any time," she replied. She let his eyes hold hers for a moment. "About eight?"

"I'll be there," he told her.

The clock seemed to stand still after she left. He had dinner at the hotel but he couldn't eat for thinking of her. The evening was unseasonably mild for that time of year. He walked for an hour, trying to reduce his mind to some semblance of ordered thinking. Why hadn't he gone while there was time? He couldn't run now. He'd have to tell her the truth. But only about his own mistakes, nothing about the one her father had made.

On arriving at the house, he had a brief glimpse of Tony's mother at a parlor window. He had a great respect for Celia Oatman. Charlie had always been something of a stuffed shirt, but not her. If there was such a thing as "quality" in a Wyoming cow town, she was it, with her kindly, unostentatious generosity and forthrightness. He saw all of her virtues reflected in Tony.

Continuing on back to the studio, he saw lights burning within. In answer to his knock, Tony called to him to enter. He found her kneeling at the fireplace, trying to get the logs to burning.

"Old Martin must have brought in some green wood," she complained. "This fireplace doesn't usually smoke." She got to her feet, replacing the fire screen. "I was going to have everything cozy and be my prettiest for you . . . Look at my hands!"

"If you were any prettier, I couldn't stand it," he said. He offered her a handkerchief. "Maybe this will help."

They stood facing each other for a long moment, their eyes saying things that made words unnecessary.

An iron band seemed to tighten about Rocky's heart. For Tony, the world was suddenly standing still.

"Rocky——!" she cried, reaching for him with her arms, her lips tremulous. He caught her and held her off, fighting himself now.

"Oh, darling, don't be angry with me for running away!" she pleaded in her innocence. "I had to go. It wasn't easy for me stay away . . . I had to prove something to myself, Rocky. Hold me close and tell me you love me!"

He gazed at her fondly, and then said in a tone more sober and earnest than she had ever heard him use, "I love you, Tony—better than life itself. But I have something to say to you. When you hear it, you won't want my love."

Even though she thought she understood what he meant, her cheeks paled. "You're going away—is that it? I heard you were leaving."

He shook his head. "That's only part of it. You'll wish I had gone. You told me once that there was something about me—you didn't know just what—that you were afraid of."

"It was foolish of me to say it," she interjected. "There was no reason——"

"No, it wasn't foolish. You were dead right. There was something."

"Rocky, what are you saying?" she cried, fear taking hold of her in earnest.

"Tony—you remember that night in California—on the beach at the Cliff House?"

"I shall never forget it as long as I live. You took

what didn't belong to you that night, Rocky. It's all yours now. All my love."

"I told you something about myself that night. You said you'd like to have me fill you in on the details . . . Well, that's what I'm going to do. I told you I bought a ranch and was going to raise bucking horses for the rodeos. It was in Wyoming, in the foothills of the Big Horns. I gave my pardners what money I had and they pulled out to buy horses. They didn't come back."

"They ran off with your money, you mean?"

"Yeh. I didn't think so at first. They were gone a long time. Winter settled down. I knew by then that I was holding the bag. I had plenty of grub. I figured I'd set out the winter, let the bank have the ranch in the spring and start drifting. One day two strangers rode in. One of them had a gunshot wound in his shoulder. They gave me the old story about an accident. It didn't fool me; I knew they'd had a brush with the law. I took them in and did a little buckshot surgery on the one with the slug in his shoulder. I had someone to share my misery now. The two of them stayed on all winter, and we got pretty well acquainted."

"They were outlaws, of course." Tony couldn't have told why, but some sixth sense warned her where this was leading.

"In a two-bit way—a couple of old Jaspers who were as down on their luck as I was. To make a long story short, I threw in with them. One day we rode into Boulder City and stuck up the bank."

"No!" Tony cried. She fell back and stared at him aghast. "You can't mean it, Rocky!"

"I'm filling you in," he said grimly and without inflection.

He told her how he and his companions had rendezvoused in Denver and how Haze and Pat had come to their death.

"That left me at the crossroads," he continued. "I knew it was up to me to stick to that life or turn my back on it forever. A copy of *Boulder City Mercury* came into my hands. I saw something about Rita Warren and her horse Hannibal, which was running in California. I put a few dollars on him. I won. That decided me; the next day, I was on my way back to Boulder City to make a fresh start."

"Father—did he suspect who you were?" Tony's throat was so tight she spoke with difficulty.

"I told him. He—he did a lot for me, Tony. In a business way, that is."

"Father made a deal with you? You—you were to repay the money when you made good?"

"Yeh. Yeh that was it." The lie didn't come easy, but he had to save Charlie Oatman's good name. "He never figured I might become interested in you. That was going too far. He didn't like it."

Tony thought she was beginning to understand her father's strangely contradictory attitude toward Rocky. Her knees felt weak and she leaned against the back of a chair to steady herself.

"You know the truth now," Rocky got out desperately. "You can see what I meant when I said I should have pulled out long ago. I don't want to put any shame on you, Tony. I'll pull up stakes and go tomorrow. Or, if you want to turn me over to Ty or the District Attorney, that'll be okay with me."

"No!" she cried, anguish tearing at her. "I don't want you to go, Rocky! You're my life—everything! You have money; you can make full restitution. I want you to face it, darling. I'll stand by you, and no shame will come to me."

"Tony—you don't know what you'd be doing to yourself! This town will be rocked to its heels if I say a word!"

"I don't care, Rocky! We'll live it down, darling! After all you've done for Boulder City and this part of Wyoming, no twelve men could be found who'd say you were guilty. No judge—not even Ira Bonfils, and he's never forgiven you for taking Rita Warren away from him—could refuse to offer you clemency." A thought flashed across her mind that shook her. "What about those other things you did with those two men?"

"They weren't important. Nobody got hurt; nobody lost any money. We were flat broke when we hit Boulder City."

"Thank God!" she cried. "You've beaten back to honesty and respectability. I'm proud of you, Rocky! Prouder than I ever was!"

His amazement grew as he gazed at her, his heart in his eyes. "You mean that, Tony? You really mean it?"

"I mean it, darling! We go on together from this moment!"

She was in his arms then, and the fireplace continued to smoke unnoticed.

Renegade by Ramsay Thorne

27 million Americans can't read a bedtime story to a child.

It's because 27 million adults in this country simply can't read.

Functional illiteracy has reached one out of five Americans. It robs them of even the simplest of human pleasures, like reading a fairy tale to a child.

You can change all this by joining the fight against illiteracy.

Call the Coalition for Literacy at toll-free **1-800-228-8813** and volunteer.

Volunteer Against Illiteracy. The only degree you need is a degree of caring.

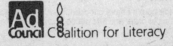

Ad Council Coalition for Literacy